THE
LIAISON

Book One in
The Desert Willow Series

NAT BURNS

BELLA
BOOKS
2018

Bella Books, Inc.
P.O. Box 10543
Tallahassee, FL 32302

First Bella Books Edition 2018

Editor: Medora MacDougall
Cover Designer: Judith Fellows

ISBN: 978-1-59493-587-9

Other Bella Books by Nat Burns

The Book of Eleanor
Family Issue
House of Cards
Identity
Lights of the Heart
Nether Regions
Poison Flowers
The Quality of Blue
Two Weeks in August

Acknowledgments

I'd like to acknowledge the wonderful original inhabitants of the New Mexico desert. They are a strong, interesting People with a fascinating culture. If I have offended any of the Native Peoples of this Land of Enchantment, it was totally unintentional as they have my highest regard.

About the Author

Nat Burns once lived for twenty-five years in an 1895 farmhouse. It was on almost two hundred acres of land in Central Virginia and was extremely isolated.

There were a lot of unexplained lights in the sky during her years there.

She now lives in New Mexico where there are *still* a lot of unexplained lights in the sky.

www.natburns.org or www.natburns.com

Dedication

A lot of people have helped in the creation of this book—my book club and my writing club members listened to me drone on endlessly about it, my beloved Chris read it after each new iteration, and the museums in the western part of the state offered a wealth of helpful information.

The scenery of New Mexico contributed greatly to this book, as well as the (possible) alien sightings and landings that (may) have happened here.

EVENT HORIZON

Sudden lightning flashed repeatedly, creating an interlaced gold and white harlequin pattern across the bright blue New Mexico sky. The staccato blazes of energy stopped abruptly as a harsh ripping sound echoed across the desert. A striped whiptail lizard scrabbled away and under a rock just as an opening, a vertical slash, appeared in the sky and hung suspended above the sandy scrubland. The slash vibrated and an ebony craft was birthed out into hot air that still bore the essence of ozone from the lightning. Spinning, the egg-shaped ship settled gracefully onto the sand, the motion not even raising one grain of dust.

Lightning returned, but this time it stayed contained within the sheltering arms of a dry grotto nearby, a large arching overhang of brown and tan stone. Spears of energy crackled as it formed into a sizeable ball of light. The ball hovered mid-grotto until a slit opened in the ship. At that point, the particles of light scattered, seeming to disperse into the very essence of the rock framing the grotto. The clear crystals embedded in the rock glowed for a long moment and then the light vanished.

A dun, bulbous head protruded from the side of the ship. A wizened lead-colored body—naked but featureless—trailed through the slit and a small alien creature jumped onto the sandy earth. A second, then a third similar form followed, and the trio stepped away from the ship. The craft spun once and faded completely from sight.

As they stood there, chests heaving as though trying to breathe unfamiliar air, one of the creatures paused and turned back to study the rock grotto some three hundred feet away. Huge dark eyes narrowed as its small slit-like mouth twisted. It lifted one long, gnarled finger and pointed toward the rocky outcropping and the rock frame lit once, brightly, as if beckoning. The creature's compadres turned as one and stared in the direction indicated. They remained that way for several moments. All was still. Even the desert wind paused in its blowing. Then a sudden wind returned, driving gritty sand across their pale, wrinkled skin and breaking the momentary lull.

One of the creatures shuffled awkwardly to one side and shoved a medium-sized boulder out of its way. The auburn, dust-coated rock rolled away along the desert floor as though made of paper. The striped whiptail lizard, which had been hiding underneath, turned to face the possible threat, its mouth open in a quiet hiss. The alien leaned forward, its rounded head cocked to one side as though studying the lizard. The whiptail moved one step back as the creature absently lifted a nearby rock. Nonchalantly, the alien slammed the rock onto the small reptile.

As the rock pounded onto the lizard, all three aliens closed their eyes, heads tilted back as though enjoying the experience together.

The solo alien, as if curious to see what he had wrought, dipped one bony, overlong finger into the remains. He lifted the finger and examined it as he lumbered back to the other two.

The creatures, grouped together once more, turned as one toward the shimmering high-rises of downtown Albuquerque looming in the distance. They communicated in a brief blast of chittering language and then ambled briskly across the hot, cactus- and juniper-speckled sand toward the heart of the city.

CHAPTER ONE

"I'm glad you're dead, Dad. There. I've said it. Are you happy?"

Lilianne Dawson paced restlessly across the sparse, closely shorn grass of the newly crafted family cemetery. Her steps were resonating and powerful. She paused and stared with a severe gaze at her father's simple headstone.

Denny (Duck) Dawson
August 20, 1948–March 12, 2018
Lieutenant General
United States Air Force

"What did you expect? That leaving me the ranch would make up for all those years of practically ignoring me?"

The pacing resumed and her spread hands, held below her waist, gestured as if pushing down air.

"Nope, not gonna happen. In fact…you know what? Yep, I'm gonna sell it. Sell it all and hightail it out of here as fast as I can. You just watch me. And….and there's nothing you can do about it. How does that feel?"

She paused in pacing and in speech, chest heaving to capture breath as she waited, listening. Of course, there was no response. Lily sighed.

"Just as well," she muttered.

"Miss Lil? We need to get on back now. Miss has rung the bell and that means dinner is ready for us."

Landon Kya'nah—her Lanny—stood at a respectful distance, on the perimeter of the wooden cemetery fencing. His worn felt hat was held in both hands and he turned it nervously, making it resemble the slow propeller of a biplane.

Lily gazed at him absently. Sudden remorse blossomed in her. How would she tell Lanny and his capable wife, Sage, that their lifetime of service would no longer be needed at Good Neighbor Ranch? That they would have to move from their home of almost twenty years? The sorrow was tinged with doubt. Could she really sell the sprawling New Mexico ranch that her father had loved so dearly?

She jutted out her chin stubbornly. It wasn't as if the ranch was all that productive. Sure, they made some money from the sale of scrawny beef cattle, but she had always marveled that her father had made any profit at all, especially when she and her mother had still lived with him.

She walked slowly toward Lanny, the sun hot against the thin T-shirt material on her back.

It must have been her father's salary from the consulting position he'd maintained after leaving military work that allowed him to continue to hold on to the ranch. And had allowed Lily and her mother to live well in Florida after they'd left New Mexico. After they'd left her father. She grimaced.

"Miss Lil." Lanny nodded his head respectfully. "Sorry to take you from your father but you know how Miss is when she has her mind set. Miss's bell says it's time to eat, it's time to eat."

Lily studied the ranch foreman's mahogany-colored, smooth features and smiled fondly at him. In some ways, Lanny had been more a father to her than her own father had. And Sage certainly more a mother than her own mother, Sandy.

"I remember it well, Lanny. Don't you worry about that."

Lanny chuckled and tucked his head as they walked toward the ranch house. After about a quarter of a mile, he adroitly swept his hat onto his head.

"Mind the goat heads," he muttered absently.

Lily dropped her gaze and stepped past the pervasive, burr-filled weed just in time. Puncturevine, or goat head as it was known, was the bane of a rancher's existence. The beautiful, golden-flowering weed produced spiny seedpods after blooming, burrs that badly injured the legs, mouths, and digestive tracts of livestock. The leaves also contained a nitrate level high enough to poison them. Not to mention what the plant did to the skin of the ranch hands unfortunate enough to encounter the scattered burrs in late summer.

"Thanks, Lanny. I sure don't miss them in Florida," she said.

"The desert is all about surviving," he reminded her. "Florida's wet. It's easier."

Lily's thoughts flew to the run-down city she lived near, filled with gangs and thievery. Most days she was more than glad to ride the bus into town to her waitress job because so many of her coworker's cars had been broken into. Or had been carjacked with no regard for the driver's well-being.

She glanced west toward the distant Zuni mountain range, knowing that there were probably only a handful of people living between Good Neighbor Ranch and that ridge. Maybe this was a good thing.

"So what's changed in the five years we've been gone, Lanny?" she asked quietly as they stepped into the paddock north of the house. She remembered hanging over this fence, watching as Lanny handled new horses, getting them under control and trained as cow horses. She looked at him again, admiring anew the copper-like sleekness of his Native American skin. He was wearing his usual outfit, thick, worn jeans and a button-down, long-sleeved cotton shirt. She had a sudden urge to grasp his long, heavy black hair in her hands as she had when still a child and he had carried her from place to place. The remembered smell of him inundated her—sweat, wood smoke, and liniment.

"Been slow here. We had rain three weeks ago. Ran in the arroyos." His expression when he glanced at her was subtly chastising.

Lily felt foolish immediately for initiating small talk with the foreman, who she knew had no need for it. Not that Lanny wasn't friendly or sociable, he simply had no use for inane chatter to fill silence. Silence was not a problem. It was not a void that needed to be filled.

They continued in that silence and Lily let a sigh of peace escape. Silence was a good thing, a restful thing. She'd forgotten that in the noisy, busy life she now led.

Approaching the long, low ranch house, Lily felt memory buoy her again as it had when she'd arrived earlier that afternoon. The memories were good ones, mostly. It had been hard saying good-bye to her one and only lengthy childhood home, the departure brought about by her parents' grim divorce following her final year of high school. She had known, in that moment of parting, that she'd lost something beyond important, something she could never again reclaim.

Yet here she was again—but forever changed—hardened by circumstance and time. The ranch, though still beautiful, had changed too. It could never hold the same magic for her that it had before. Looking at it through new, mature eyes, she could see that it was little more than a desert outpost. Well-maintained, yes, but surrounded by miles and miles of scrub desert. She gazed out over the west pasture and saw the black dots of grazing Criollo cows off in the heat-wavering distance. Did she want to live in such an isolated spot? Of course not.

She fingered the cell phone in her jeans pocket, wanting to check it for messages, but she wasn't ready for Lanny's scorn should he see her do it.

They mounted the steps to the front porch, Lanny's boots echoing a familiar tune from her childhood. Sage, standing at the partially opened screen door, was yet one more surrealistic memory. For a brief moment, Lily wondered if she were indeed truly, physically, back in Morris, New Mexico.

"Well, took you two long enough," Sage said in her strange, song-like English that touched Lily somewhere deep inside every time she heard it. "Didn't you hear the bell?"

Lanny grunted and held the door for Lily. She brushed past Sage, pausing to grin at her to defuse the older woman's frown. It took a few seconds, but Sage's lips began their slow curve upward.

"Get on with you," she said, playfully swatting Lily's rear. "Wash your hands, both of you. Lord knows what you've gotten into."

Lanny grinned and shoved Lily to one side as they stepped into the mudroom next to the kitchen and stopped at the deep utility sink to wash their hands.

"Hey, you married her," Lily muttered as she focused on her fingernails.

Heavenly smells were coming from the kitchen, chief among them Lily's favorite—fresh, homemade bread.

"And no regrets," he replied, handing her a towel.

They passed into the kitchen and Lily took her customary seat at the scarred wooden table as if no time had passed. There was a formal dining room less than ten feet away but it had only been used when her mother had insisted or when visitors dined with them. Most meals at the ranch happened at this overlarge, shellacked kitchen table, crafted from weathered and bowed cottonwood. Quite often it had been only Lily and her mother, her father too busy working and Lanny, and Sage, of course, never daring to eat with Sandy Weiss Dawson.

"And your father?" Sage asked as she brought large bowls of beef stew to the table.

Lily's mouth watered. It had been a long time since she'd had Sage's excellent cooking. "Well, we didn't have a lot to talk about," Lily replied with a sigh.

Sage pressed against her back as she leaned to place a bowl of stew in front of Lanny. "Was the stone okay? We just got the basic one after…"

"I know," Lily said. "I'm sorry I didn't come out to help with the arrangements. What you chose is fine. Thank you."

Sage took her seat and the three lowered their heads in a moment of silence.

The first mouthful of stew caused Lily to moan aloud. "Oh, my God, this is good. I don't know what you do, Saysay, but I've never tasted stew this good anywhere from here to Florida."

Sage chuckled and pulled off a chunk of homemade bread and handed it to Lily. "It's made with love and other good stuff," she explained.

Lily smiled her thanks and reached for the butter knife.

"Fresh beef," Lanny offered as he accepted the bread Sage handed him. "Makes it special."

"That could be," Lily agreed around a mouthful of bread.

"Your mother?" Sage asked gently. She averted her eyes.

Lily chewed and swallowed before answering. "The same." She lowered her head. "She does manage to keep the trailer park running. She doesn't start drinking until late afternoon and that seems to work for her."

"What do you do? Waitress?" Lanny asked.

"I still waitress at Clay's Eatery. In the historic part of town. I get a lot of tourist tips and it's enough for me."

"You still look after her, though?" Sage sounded worried that Lily would abandon her mother.

"Oh, of course. She pretty much needs me to help her, especially in the evenings. I work the morning and early afternoon shifts at the café. Got lucky with that."

Sage nodded. "Yes, lucky."

Lily took another bite of stew and let the hot, salty goodness linger on her tongue for a few seconds. "Guess Dad decided Mama would drink the property up. That's why he left it to me?"

Sage nodded and studied Lily pensively. "Your father loved you. Never had the time, but he did cherish you."

Lily grunted ruefully. "Yeah, he cherished the thought of me. The reality? Not so much."

Sage stirred dismissively and became keenly interested in her own bowl of stew.

Lanny reached for a second chunk of bread. "Will you move back?"

Lily sighed and sat back, chewing thoughtfully. Panic filled her, but she knew she couldn't lie to the sweet countenances studying her. "No, I don't think so. There's no work here for me or for Mama."

Sage placed her spoon carefully on the table. "But the ranch. Who will run the ranch?"

Lily could only shake her head as her eyes filled with unwanted tears. She knew selling the ranch would be a huge step, but she didn't want to prolong the misery wrought by her father. Being here was painful and brought back all those memories of her father's back to her as he walked away, busy with something else. Something besides her.

Lanny stood abruptly, painstakingly shoved his chair under the table and left the kitchen without a word. Lily stared at his abandoned dinner with her heart crawling up into her throat. His disapproval lingered like an unpleasant odor.

What did they expect of her? Her life lay elsewhere now. Anger rose in her, and ignoring the tears that filled her eyes, she lifted an annoyed gaze to Sage.

But Sage's eyes were turned toward the window above the sink. She was chewing thoughtfully, her mind obviously very far away and focused on something different from the here and now.

CHAPTER TWO

I feel like crap, Lily typed into her phone.

Dinner was over and Lily had retreated to the front porch after Sage had refused her offer of help with the dishes. Now she was finally able to communicate with her friends.

R u sure u wanna sell? Diana texted. *I mean, u do love that place.*

Bastard's place, Lily wrote. *Bt feel bad fr sage n lanny.*

Tru but u r lttg him win.

No. Kickng his butt. He rlly lovd it here.

Carrie says hi.

Carrie was Diana's girlfriend of the month. Lily couldn't even remember what she looked like.

Hi back. Everything ok at café?

Sure. No probs. Leonard grabbed my ass.

LOL. Grab his back.

K. Mom is ok. Went by yesterday.

Good-thx.

Welcome. Nd me, txt me.

Wrk smarter nt harder, Lily wrote in her usual sign-off to Diana.

Lily scrolled through her phone and dealt with a few emails before making the screen inactive and resting her head back on the rocking chair. She tucked her phone away and closed her eyes. She could almost smell the scent of frying potatoes and grilled meat and onions that permeated the café where she worked. It had become very strange for her to be away from work or from the trailer park where she lived. She knew she should text or email her mother again but knew that by this time, Sandy was well into the maudlin phase of her inebriation and Lily just didn't feel up to that. She leaned forward and fished a pack of cigarettes from her pocket. She shook one out and lit it with the lighter kept stored in the cellophane sleeve of the pack. She inhaled, the harsh smoke invading her lungs and wakening her anew.

Wondering what her next move should be, she stared at the porch ceiling. She needed to call a realtor to list the property. That would probably be the first priority. She also needed to ride the range and make sure everything was okay with the land and the fencing. Not that she was worried—Lanny was an excellent crew chief.

Then she needed to get up with Margie to find out the status of the livestock and who would be a potential buyer if the property listed with or without livestock. She sighed and flicked the ash off her cigarette. There was a lot to do and the two weeks she'd scheduled would fly by. She could stay longer, if necessary. Diana had a friend covering for Lily at the café, but she didn't feel safe leaving her mom alone that long. It would be her luck that Sandy would burn the trailer park down and then they'd *have* to move back to New Mexico.

A sudden weight on her legs startled her and her eyes snapped downward. Twit, the orange-striped tom she had brought home from the annual harvest fair eight years ago, stared up at her with brilliant topaz eyes. He had gotten huge under Sage's excellent care.

"Well, hello, where have you been?" she said, pulling him close in a prolonged hug.

Twit head-butted her chin and a purr rattled the broad chest under her petting hands. She had forgotten about Twit. Relocating him, a free-roaming ranch cat, was going to be tough. Lily sighed and leaned forward to bury her face in Twit's soft fur. Tears welled and dampened the fur against her eyes. Twit continued to purr, his tail entwining about her arm as if for comfort.

No, not going to be easy, none of it. After Sage notified her about her father's sudden death, Lily had been stunned but uncaring. She'd lost herself in her daily routine, not bothering to consider it further. Then, after being contacted by the lawyer handling the estate, she'd been forced to deal. And she hated that. Hated that she had to be drawn back into this circle that she had so forcibly removed herself from.

She crushed out the cigarette on the sole of her shoe and laid the butt aside.

Leaving the ranch five years ago had been like ripping her heart out, but she had quickly toughened and moved past the binding she felt to the land and people here. Being forced to take care of her mother had helped. Sandy had been a bundle of fury and regret, bouncing between the two emotions like a well-played handball. During the past few years, with only his holiday cards and monthly checks, as if from faraway, distant relatives, Lily and her mother had done well. Had forgotten well. To be thrust back into that emotional torrent now, reminding her of what she had lost, was bordering on a type of insanity. Lily was a master at compartmentalizing her life and this…this death of the father…had no compartment.

Steps sounding on the floorboards inside caused Lily to raise her head and wipe her eyes on the shoulder of her T-shirt. She had to stay strong and see this through. She needed to regain control, to regain sanity in her life. She cuddled Twit up onto her shoulder where he purred against her ear.

"Beautiful evening," Sage said as she stepped onto the porch.

Silence fell between them. Sage was another Native who needed no small talk. Lily's cell vibrated in her pocket, but she ignored it. Probably her mother.

They remained that way a long time, a New Mexico ranch tableau, Lily and Twit in the rocking chair and Sage standing at the porch railing, eyes surveying the scrubland surrounding the house.

"You can take your pa's room for as long as you're here," she said as she settled into the rocking chair next to Lily.

"My old room's fine," Lily replied absently, hand resting on Twit's rump. Her gaze was on the changing sunset that was lending ribbons of pastel to the mountains and the western sky.

"I made up the room for you," Sage reiterated firmly. They sat silently as the sun lowered below the horizon and dusk claimed the desert. After some time, a chill swept across Lily. Sage must have felt it too, for she rose and pulled her ancient, dark blue cardigan close.

"Good night, sweet girl," she said, leaning to kiss Lily's forehead. "The room's all ready for you and I unpacked everything. Don't forget to lock the front door."

"You're not staying here?" She hated the alarm in her voice.

"No, Little Lil," Sage said patiently, moving to stand at the top of the porch steps. "I'm going to sleep in the guest house, next to my husband, like I have for forty years. You'll be fine and I'll be back in the morning before breakfast. Go, sleep. It's been a long day."

Lily stiffened her shoulders. "Thank you, Saysay. I love you."

Sage waved over her shoulder as she descended the steps and moved across the front yard. She was backlit by interior lights against the deep purple sky as she hoisted herself into her old dented pickup. The truck, using no headlights, slowly lumbered away along the wide dirt drive.

Lighting another cigarette, Lily sat watching the now cloudless night sky until a sly stirring in a clump of nearby brush worried her and sent her inside, Twit at her heels. Coyote often hunted rabbit near the house and she wanted the two of them to have no part of that. Once inside, she locked the door and sighed at the emptiness of the large home—very different from the cramped two-bedroom mobile home she and her mother lived in now. This house was like a presence around her—a creature that inexplicably frightened her. She lingered at the door and recalled a time when it had been filled with family. Once it had even been a happy family. She frowned at the dimness as Twit meandered toward the darkened kitchen, probably seeking the midnight snack Sage, no doubt, invariably left for him.

Lily strode along the long hallway leading to the master bedroom, switching off lights as she passed them. At the door to what once had been her parents' bedroom, she paused, old restrictions ballooning in her brain. She shook them off and pressed open the door.

Sage had left the bedside lamps on and the room was almost cheerful, even welcoming. She closed the door and moved silently into the master bath. Sage had arranged Lily's toiletries in her usual efficient manner and Lily debated showering. Fatigue won out and she merely brushed her teeth and washed her face instead.

Yawning as she reentered the bedroom, she realized how tired she'd become. The idea of selling the ranch was eating away at her, and even after she'd burrowed beneath the Russian sage-scented blankets, her own thoughts berated her. And although she expected to be awake for hours, sleep came quickly and blessedly gave her peace.

CHAPTER THREE

A noise woke her—a small sigh. Actually, several small sighs. Later she would wonder how many hesitant sighs had sounded before she rose to full consciousness.

She opened one eye. Then both as she sensed a presence and fully realized there was someone in the room with her. The small figure moved, and Lily, heart racing, sat up, the sheet rocketing away from her body.

It was a small boy. No more than four or five. Gasping, Lily tried to control her breathing and steady her heartbeat, a hand pressed to her chest.

It was just a child. A small child.

He stood still finally, stopping his frantic movement around the room. He regarded her with large, calm eyes beneath a mop of dark, curly hair. She studied him. He was wearing pale, beige flannel pajamas with small brown trains scattered across them. His face was round, cherubic, with a small dimple below his full lips. His large brown eyes watched her warily.

"Hello," she said quietly.

"Hello," he responded.

They regarded one another in silence until Lily spoke again. "Where's your mother?"

The boy studied her in silence for most of a full minute before replying. "Where's the duck?"

Lily wrinkled her brow, trying to understand. "Did you lose a toy?" she asked. Surely he didn't mean her father. Only his air force cronies called Denny Dawson by the nickname Duck.

The child had to be one of Sage's grandchildren. They popped up on the ranch from time to time but not usually in the middle of the night. She glanced at the clock. Almost four in the morning. Crazy. There was no way she was taking him to Sage and Lanny's house now. She sighed loudly.

"Okay. What's your name, little guy?"

"Cory."

The boy moved closer and stuck his right thumb into his mouth. He was adorable. He stepped until he was right next to her, and he gazed at her with speculative but sleepy eyes. Without thinking about it, she reached under his arms and a sudden static shock caused her to cry out and jerk her hands away. Smiling and shaking her head to comfort him, she tried again, gingerly, this time lifting him onto the bed. She pulled the blankets loose and then tucked them about both of them. They lay curled on their sides, knees almost touching. His eyes closed and he smiled around his thumb.

"We'll worry about getting you back home later. I just hope they aren't out looking for you," she whispered sleepily.

He reached out and took her forearm in his heated hand, then quickly let it go.

"So, that's what happened. We searched..." he muttered quietly as she drifted off. The words struck her as odd, but by then she was too close to Morpheus's realm to turn back.

The bright light of a New Mexico morning came insistently through the sheer white curtains covering the east-facing windows in her father's bedroom. No wonder he had risen so early every day. Lily turned her back to the windows and adjusted her pillow, hoping for a few more hours of sleep. Her mind betrayed her, however, and she suddenly remembered the child. She sat up and squinted into the sunlight. The other side of the bed was empty, only a small indentation in the pillow proving the little boy hadn't been a dream she'd created.

In the bathroom, she stared into sleep blurred hazel-brown eyes under tousled, natural light blond hair. Once again, she spent a moment marveling at how little she looked like either of her parents. Her father had dark hair and blue eyes and her mother had dark blond hair with brown eyes. Maybe she really was adopted but everyone was afraid to tell her.

After a refreshing shower, Lily dressed then followed the inviting scents of bacon and coffee into the cool, dim kitchen. Sage, standing at the stove, looked up as she entered.

"Good morning, Little Lil. How was the sleep?" She placed a plate bearing scrambled eggs, hash browns, and crisp bacon on the table and indicated for Lily to sit. Lily did as bidden and tucked into the delicious food. When Sage brought her three small, buttery pancakes, she lit into those as well. Sometime later, fully sated, she sat back and gazed at Sage who sat across from her, coffee mug in hand. Twit came into the room and did figure eights around her feet.

"That was sooo good. Thank you. I really do miss your cooking. It's so much better than the diner food I get usually."

Sage smiled, her dark eyes glinting in a random shaft of morning light. The kitchen was at the back of the house, on the northern, mesa side, so by the time daylight arrived through those windows, the day was well underway. The sound of men working outside the house drifted in.

"Are they working on the yard?" she asked, sipping her own coffee.

"Mmm. Clearing rocks," Sage replied.

"From the mesa?"

Sage nodded. "A quake. Two weeks ago. Shook rocks loose."

"Wow. Was there much damage back there?" Lily picked at the bacon crumbs remaining on her plate as she awaited the answer.

"Back of the storage shed dented in and part of the fence down. I knew you were coming so I didn't write you about it," she replied.

Lily pushed her plate away so she'd stop picking at it. "That's fine, Saysay. I know you and Lanny have it under control."

Her thoughts whirled like a tornado. Pulling and pushing. Yes, Lanny and Sage had always had the best interests of the ranch at heart. Asking them to pack up and move away would be a brutal removal of everything they held dear. Lily sighed, swamped with new guilt.

"Did Cory make it home okay?" she asked, seeking a distraction from her thoughts.

"Cory?"

"Oh, I assumed he was one of your grandkids."

Sage was watching her keenly. "What are you saying? All mine are up at the village this time of year. School still."

"But…" Lily hesitated. Had she dreamed it after all?

"Is this someone you saw yesterday?" Sage asked.

"No, I…" Lily shrugged. "Last night…well, early this morning. Maybe I dreamed it."

Sage sat back thoughtfully, her eyes never leaving Lily's face. "Cory?"

Lily nodded and shrugged again. "I don't know. It was a long day…"

"How did he look?" An odd, secretive smile played at the corners of Sage's lips as she leaned to gently pull on one of Twit's ears. Twit purred in pleasure and head-butted her hand.

Lily watched her, trying to get the joke. "A little boy, young, pre-school age, dark hair and eyes, like your bunch."

"Ahh." Sage rose and moved to the sink. "Our people say that the dreams speak to us. We are bound to listen."

"What do you think this dream was trying to tell me? That I want a little boy to take care of? I don't *think* so."

Sage chuckled and watched the workmen through the short window above the sink as her hands automatically washed the dishes. "Guess we'll wait and see," she answered quietly.

Lily's phone, on the table next to her plate, lit and an automated news brief crawled slowly across the screen. There was a nationwide flu outbreak that seemed to have originated in the Southwest.

"Hmm, flu. I hate flu," Lily muttered. It seemed someone always brought it into the diner and laid it right at her door.

"What's that?" Sage dried her hands on a red-checked dishtowel.

Lily darkened the phone. "Just a flu outbreak. Guess we'll be obsessively washing our hands again."

"Your machine told you that?" Sage asked, indicating Lily's cell.

Lily sighed deeply and, grinning, rolled her eyes as though in exasperation.

CHAPTER FOUR

The thick muscles under the velvet skin covering the flanks of her horse, Shakey, contracted and expanded beneath her thighs, causing a gentle, lulling motion as she rode a good portion of the twenty-two hundred acres of Good Neighbor Ranch. She fondled the soft skin of Shakey's neck and tangled her fingers in the thick, coarse mane, remembering the mare's premature birth. Seeing the sleek, russet foal sliding from her mother's birth canal had been one of the most thrilling and terrifying moments of Lily's life. When the filly had hit the hay-strewn stall, young Lily had covered her mouth with both hands, overcome with awe and tenderness. It had been such a harsh, laborious entry into the world. The tiny newborn, unfazed by her impact with the ground, raised her triangular head and gazed sleepily at Lily as if saying good morning. That moment was when nine-year-old Lily fell in love with the little foal.

Gaining proprietorship of the filly had been another issue, but Lily had characteristically dug in her heels and refused to be swayed from bonding with the new arrival. Thus, Shakey had become her first steady companion, and they had shared a wealth of adventure exploring the rolling desert plateaus of their new home.

Riding the ranch acreage today brought back those memories with bittersweet fondness. Pre-divorce, it had been the expanding of a young girl's world. During the divorce, it had been her solace and solitude. As she had then, Lily leaned forward now and buried her face in the hay-scented hair of Shakey's neck, thankful that the horse had remembered her after such a long absence. She tightened her thighs expertly, still knowing how to cling to the mare's bare back, her hands entwined into the long tan mane for safety. Shakey responded as usual, lowering her neck and turning her head to nuzzle Lily briefly. They moved forward and Lily closed her eyes, trusting Shakey to take them where she would.

Tough thoughts ripped and rebounded through Lily's mind. Selling the ranch would essentially end a way of life. More than two dozen ranch hands would lose their positions, half of them their home. Then there was Lanny and Sage. Where would they go? Back to Sky Village, she supposed, the Acoma Pueblo located midway between Good Neighbor and Grants. It was where they'd grown up and still had family.

"Maybe the new owner will keep them all on," Lily muttered against Shakey's neck.

Shakey stopped abruptly as a harsh sound pushed against Lily's ears, raising the small hairs on her arms and neck. Lily lifted her head slowly, her heart hammering in her throat.

"Back, Shakey," she whispered hoarsely as she gently tugged the mane. "Back away."

Her eyes roamed the parched earth in front of them, slowly moving to the right. There he was, thick-bodied and coiled protectively. She changed the pressure of her tug on the horse's mane, pulling to the left. Shakey responded slowly, moving her hooves one at a time. This was not their first encounter with a rattler, but this one was huge, a true grandfather, and his reach would be long. The rattles sounded again as his tongue flicked repeatedly, in and out of his broad triangular head, eyes glinting in sunlight. In a moment of surreal clarity, Lily was able to count the extended rattles at the end of his body, roughly one for each year. That indicated that this one was old, more than twelve years.

"We mean you no harm, grandparent," Lily said as she continued to ease the horse back and to the left. She slowly took off her broad-brimmed cloth hat in a gesture of respect and muttered an Acoma charm that Lanny had taught her, to be on the safe side.

They sat still a long time, Shakey's heavy bellows-like breathing the only sound. After what seemed like half an hour, the rattlesnake shook his tail once more, as if in indignation, then languidly crossed the dirt in front of them. Lily watched his fleshy, muscular form move away and breathed out a sigh of relief.

"Wow," she said unevenly, as she resettled her hat on her sun-heated blond hair. "Wouldn't Sage have liked having his skin on her altar?"

Shakey swung her head in agreement and they moved on, crisis averted.

The ruddy mare must have been thirsty after riding the fences for she turned left, heading toward Dillon's Run, the narrow, deep crevice creek that ran at the foot of Moon Mesa. Sliding off to let her drink, Lily stared up at the rocky slide defining the mesa and could keenly taste the remembered chalk smell of dry soil and hot, crumbled rock. Gazing left, she saw the ranch house off in the distance, marking the bottom end of the mesa. From this distance, the house looked serene, even beautiful. Lily had hoped for that aura in the beginning, when they had moved from Washington, DC. She'd quickly been faced with a mother separated from friends and her usual social events and a father ever increasingly tied to a phone and swamped with learning how to work a ranch. It had been a recipe for failure.

The expansive New Mexico sky was a palette of crisp blue and white as it framed the sprawling ranch, with its split rail inner fencing. Lily closed her eyes against the glare and sighed. Shakey had finished drinking from the shallow stream so Lily led her up the slight rise and toward the main road. She'd lost her desire to ride and instead wanted to walk. She had a lot of thinking to do but found herself mindlessly enjoying the brilliance of the day. Unproductively. A steady wind caressed her neck and shoulders, and she tilted her head to one side so she could relish the sensation. It had been so long since she'd been caressed by any entity, whether human or Mother Nature. The touching had stopped even before her breakup with her last girlfriend, Tawny. In many ways the distancing, both emotional and physical, had contributed to the split. No, had caused the split. And then there had been her mother's steady, predictable interference.

The sound of an approaching vehicle distracted her and she pulled Shakey's mane so that the mare would move closer to her and be calmed by her proximity. She turned and saw a faded blue truck approaching from behind them.

"Well, my golly. It's Lil! Stop this truck right now and let me hug this girl!" Margie Sweetwater exclaimed from the passenger seat. Click Sweetwater, in the driver's seat, grinned at Lily as his hefty wife scrambled from the truck and swept Lily into her arms and lifted her from the ground. Lily rolled her eyes at Click as she let go of Shakey and wrapped her arms around Margie as far as she could.

Margie pulled back and studied Lily, concern etched into her broad, dark features. "Hon, I am so sorry your father passed. I'm very sorry he was taken from all of us so soon."

"Thank you for the card you sent," Lily said, holding Margie's hand in both of hers. "It really touched me. And Mama."

"Least I could do, sweetie. Did you enjoy living down south?"

Lily nodded. "It's hot, but not like here. It's like breathing soup down there sometimes. And there's lots more people. Mean people."

Margie nodded vigorously, the loose flesh under her chin shaking. "Well, we're mighty glad you're back where you need to be. We're still your family. Where is Sandy this morning?

I have sure missed your ma. You know we had coffee every morning before ya'll moved away."

Lily's tongue suddenly felt weighted. "I...she..." Lily stammered out.

"Margie, what are you doing ta that gal? Leave her be. You got a passel of work to do and I do too."

Margie scowled at Click, impudent eyebrows wrinkling her wide forehead. "Listen, honey, we gotta go. You tell your mama to come by the office and see me. Tell her I'll keep the coffee hot." Laughing, Margie hefted her large form into the already rolling truck and waved cheerfully as she slammed the door.

Shakey stepped restlessly and Lily soothed her with hands and voice, even as she watched the truck retreat.

Damn! Lily felt an overwhelming urge to leave. To hijack one of the ranch vehicles and drive herself to the airport and never look back. As they resumed their slow walk toward the ranch house, Lily idly wondered what would happen to the property if she did walk away. She shook her head, sensing that it would be a worse disaster than her stepping up and doing what needed to be done.

CHAPTER FIVE

I feel sick, her mother texted her that evening at dinner.

Lily's phone was on the table and the screen lit briefly, showing her the message.

"Sage, where is Lanny?"

Sage looked up from her plate of roast beef, biscuits, and green chile gravy. "Said a dead tree needed cutting over east pasture. Keeping a plate warm for him."

"Hmm. I think he's avoiding me," Lily said quietly. "I guess we all need to talk about selling the property."

Sage sighed and pushed her mostly empty plate away. "Guess we do."

Lily reached out and placed her hand over Sage's. "It's not that I want to sell...I have my own life now. Mama, too. We can't come back here."

Sage watched her with placid calm. "That's not true and you know it. You don't want to come back because your father lived here."

Lily stirred uncomfortably and drew back her hand. "Not completely, although I guess that's part of it..."

"Is it money? Do you need money from the sale?"

"Mama wants the money," Lily admitted quietly. "Says Dad owes her."

"He does," Sage agreed. "That's why you need to come back here to live. That's why he left it to you, so you and your ma could have a place to live. One that was paid for."

Lily shook her head. "No, I don't think Mama would come back here. She's developed a real hatred toward this place. Most of the damage has been built up in her own mind, but that doesn't change the way she feels."

Sage shook her head. "It won't be easy. This place is worth millions but with people so poor now…"

"I know." Lily nervously chewed a thumbnail. "I don't know what I will do if it doesn't sell."

"Stay here, child!" Sage said urgently as she grabbed Lily's hand. "You can't even imagine what would happen…"

She quieted herself and sat back again. "You just need to stay here and carry on with what your father wanted you to do."

"And what is that? Beef farming? There's less and less grass every year and feed prices versus beef prices…well, you simply can't get back what you put into it."

Sage pulled her plate close and picked at the cooling, leftover food. "We can't stop you. It belongs to you."

"I…I know and, well, maybe we can find work for all the hands. Or maybe the new owner will keep everyone on…"

Sage let loose a short bark of laughter. Her deep brown eyes fixed on Lily and Lily saw so many guilt-inducing things there that she had to look away. Sage rose and picked up a short stack of mail from the counter. "Taking this to Margie before she leaves the office," she said. "Want to go?"

"No, Mama texted me. I need to see what she wants."

Sage nodded. "Leave those dishes," she said as she left the kitchen, slinging her worn, broken felt hat onto her head. The dearly familiar action pierced Lily's heart. She had forgotten that precious old hat of Saysay's.

Blinking tears from her eyes, she sat back and lifted her phone. She dialed her mother and was surprised when it was answered on the second ring.

"Lilianne?"

"Yes, Mama. What's wrong?"

"I'm sick with the flu. Got a huge headache." She sneezed into her phone as if for proof.

Lily grimaced. "Do you have a fever?"

"I don't think so, but I'm dizzy. Got the Tijuana two-step, too."

"What meds did you take? Cold medicine?" Lily rose and carried her phone through the house and out the front door. Evening was settling in and the sky was a rich mantle of magenta around the ranch. The Sandia Mountains off in the east distance glowed a dusky rose color.

"That gel cap stuff you had here. I took two of those. Didn't help much." Sandy sniffed. "And I'm thirsty. Can't get enough to drink."

Lily lit a cigarette and realized suddenly that she wasn't hearing any background noise. Was her mother alone? With no television blaring?

"What are you doing, Mama?"

"I told you, I'm goddamned sick. I'm in bed. I get dizzy, wanna puke when I get up." Her mother's impatience was evident.

Lily fell silent. She wasn't used to this situation. Though usually plagued with aches from arthritis, her mother seemed to be pickled by the booze she drank and seldom caught even a cold.

"Is anyone looking after you, Mama?"

Sandy coughed loudly, deeply. "That girl you work with was here...with that scary woman."

Lily suddenly remembered what Carrie looked like. Very masculine. Extreme butch.

"That was just her girlfriend, Carrie. Were you nice to them?"

"I don't think that's what your main concern should be, do you?" Anger tinged Sandy's voice.

"I'm sorry, Mama," Lily said with a sigh. "Do me a favor and call Lucy. Get her to come over and sit with you some."

"She's too old," Sandy said petulantly. "And she smells like burnt bacon. When are you coming home?"

Lily sighed again and chewed her bottom lip. Damn, she wanted to go hide. Her tone when she spoke was a little sharper than she had intended. "I don't know, Mama. As soon as I get all this shit dealt with here, when do you think? It's not easy getting rid of all this crap. And who but Daddy would want to buy a ranch out in the middle of nowhere like this one?"

Sandy didn't respond right away, and Lily pictured her taking a sip from her tall soda fountain glass filled with ice and vodka tonic.

"Don't drink too much with that cold medicine...it's got pain reliever in it and might hurt your liver," Lily said quietly.

"I know this is hard on you, honey. I do," Sandy finally said. "At least your father isn't there..." She paused, as if realizing the possible effect of her words. "I...I'm sorry, you..." She coughed loudly.

"Look, Mama, get some rest and let your body heal, okay? I'm gonna call George and Lucy and let them know that you're sick. You call me right away if you need anything, okay? Promise?"

"Pinkie swear," Sandy muttered, causing Lily to smile. It was a swear they'd shared often when Lily was young.

Lily signed off and immediately typed George into her contacts search engine. She called him, picturing the sweet, elderly gentleman who lived alone in Lot 2-B. She apologized for the late call but explained the situation, and he responded quickly saying that he would look after her mother and also work the front desk until Sandy was feeling better. Lily then called Lucy and was assured that Lucy, a retired nurse who lived in Lot 5-A, would pop over and care for Sandy right away.

Feeling somewhat reassured, Lily switched off the phone, sat back, and lit another cigarette as she watched the evening sun creep toward her across the desert. She heard Sage enter by the back-kitchen doorway and felt a comforting sense of peace steal across her. It was nice to let her guard down and allow these people, the family of her youth, to care for her and her surroundings. For so many years she had been the adult in her relationship with her mother. She'd worked so hard to prove her independence from her father and to provide the extras that she and her mother needed. To sit here now, hearing Sage in the kitchen, hearing the low murmurs of the ranch hands and smelling the wood smoke from their pit fire where the coffee cooked day and night, she felt complete and fully at ease. She rose, stretched thoroughly, then went into the house. She meandered slowly down the side hallway until she reached the kitchen. Impulsively, she went to Sage and pulled her into a powerful hug. Sage laid aside the dishes she'd been holding and held Lily the same way.

Lily loved the smell of Sage. It was a specific almond-scented lotion. Sage had a thing for the original version of that brand and had been using it religiously since Lily had known her. It was comforting to have her senses filled with that familiar scent and know that she was in this truly safe place.

She remembered suddenly the day that she'd left the ranch. She'd clung to Sage in much the same way then. There was no need for words. The physical connection had been enough.

CHAPTER SIX

She was dreaming that her father was talking to her, but his words were so rapid and so garbled that she couldn't make them out. As if frustrated that she couldn't understand him, he frowned at her then turned and began to walk away. She reached for his back, wanting to claw it, make it bleed so that he would know she was still there. She wanted to hear him, wanted to know what it was he wanted to tell her. Why couldn't he understand that? She began sobbing, begging him to come back to her, to talk to her. She needed his help, needed his advice.

Mouth open in a silent scream of anger and need, Lily bolted from the mattress, the blankets that had covered her coming loose and arcing through the air. She stood next to the bed, heart racing and breath rasping through her mouth. She pressed a palm to her chest and realized her face was wet with tears that she had actually shed in her sleep.

She mopped at her face with her hands and T-shirt, then sat on the side of the bed, her heart calming somewhat. She reached for the bedside lamp and switched it on. Maybe she would read for a while until the dream faded from her mind. She lifted the book she'd purloined from her father's office and reclined against the pillows with a sigh.

She lifted her eyes and screamed.

The woman sitting in her father's beat-up recliner opposite the bed lurched in alarm, her strange, silver eyes widening and her long, slender hands gripping the arms of the chair.

Lily swallowed hard and forced herself into a state of feigned calmness as she studied the woman.

"Who are you and what are you doing in my father's…in my…bedroom?"

The small figure relaxed slightly. Her voice was light and breathy, with a strange humming undertone. "We know who you are. Do you remember us? Me?"

Of course, she would have to be clinically insane, Lily thought as she reached for her phone which was plugged in and charging on the nightstand.

"It won't work, Lily, when we are here like this, in this form. You should…remember that," the woman said in a breathy sigh of regret. "Our real presence is too strong and interferes with those devices."

Lily watched her a few long seconds before unplugging her phone and activating the home screen. She tried to dial 911 but the numbers would not enter via the keyboard. Plus, the screen and digital keypad was lit white with static. She glanced up, to make sure the woman was staying put, then repeatedly pressed the area of the emergency dial button. She moaned in frustration.

"I'm sorry," the woman murmured softly. "It's the life field that surrounds us when in this form. Try it closer to the window."

"Us? What us?" Lily asked, gauging the distance to the bedroom door. She would have to pass right by the crazy woman and she wasn't sure she wanted to get that close to her. And she was in the house alone, so she couldn't call out for help.

"We are…sorry…for the passing of your…father," the woman said.

Lily peered more closely at her. There was something familiar— "Did you know my father?"

"Of course. We were…colleagues. We…worked together."

"In Washington?"

The woman nodded. "At times. But more here. This is our… headquarters."

Silence fell as the two regarded one another. Lily spoke, finally.

"Why are you here at four in the morning? Those aren't exactly business hours," she said. Had this woman and her father been having an affair? Is that why her parents divorced? The real reason?

She studied the woman. She had extremely short, white blond hair, cropped choppily, and glowing eyes that, in the light of the bedside lamp, looked almost endless in their silvery depth. She was wearing loose boxy pajamas that also appeared silverish. The material shimmered with each movement of the woman's body, as though unattached to reality.

"Time means nothing to us," the woman replied.

"Who are you?" Lily felt anger swell in her. Had this beautiful woman actually destroyed her parents' marriage?

The woman bowed her head. "They call me Eef-lin."

"Eeeeaa-afaaleen? What sort of name is that?" Lily struggled to her feet and stood facing the odd woman. The name had been pronounced with a strange hum of energy that shook her to the bone. It had awakened a bizarre, not entirely unfamiliar sensation within her.

"It is hard for your mouth to say. Duck called us Flynn. Would you like to call…me… Flynn?" The woman had tilted her head and was eyeing Lily quizzically.

"Have I met you before?" Lily asked.

She backed away until she felt the bed against her thighs. She sat gingerly on the side of the bed. Her feet were cold from the bare wooden floor. She could feel the cool but rumpled sheets beneath her palms. Her head was buzzing and she felt spacey.

Flynn nodded. "Yes. Many times, in your…youth. You went away though. A better decision for us. But now Duck…left us, too. His energy moved away from your dimension and we did not...sense it...though his is not so young. If we had known..."

"If you had known...what?" Lily felt as though she had stepped into an episode of *The Twilight Zone*. This had to be a very detailed, important dream. She tried to soak it all in so she could tell Sage about it at breakfast.

"We might have collected him. Made him part of us. He was deserving although it is seldom...done."

"Us again. Why do you speak of us? Who are you?" Lily's tolerance had just about reached its breaking point.

Flynn seemed to understand. "Lily, please hear us. I am...one small part of an...an energy...collective. We are not of your world because we care nothing for human dimensions. We left all human things behind in our infancy..."

"Right!" Lily interrupted. "And my father was concerned with this...this collective?" She inclined her head in an implied question.

Flynn looked perplexed. Or maybe frustrated. It was hard to tell with the shimmering clothing reflecting against her face. "It's...if one of us cares or has interest, we break away and follow it. We...me...I find your dimension in need. There is...compulsion to follow, to allow you to...extend."

"What the *fuck* are you talking about?" Lily said with a quick bark of disbelieving laughter.

Flynn's shimmer became more pronounced as she shifted in the chair. "Tell me, Lily. Do you know what your father was...what he did for your world?"

"Oh, man," Lily moaned. She placed a palm on either side of her head and shook it back and forth, eyes closed. "This is one hell of a dream."

Suddenly, dry, oven-like heat washed across her, so hot that she was made momentarily breathless. She opened her eyes and gasped, trying to breathe in the air, which was suddenly unbearably hot. Luckily, the heat passed quickly and she could inhale again.

Her gaze flew to the chair. It was empty.

CHAPTER SEVEN

Whoa, it was a doozie, Lily texted the next morning.

She and Twit were alone in the kitchen because it was Sage's market day. Even though she was gone, Sage had left a full breakfast for Lily on the back of the stove. It would never even occur to her to let Lily get her own breakfast.

It sounds like it, Diana answered. *But what I want to know is, was she hot?*

Lily laughed as she munched on perfectly fried, crisp bacon. *Well, yeah, in a Star Trekky kind of way, I guess. Especially when she disappeared.*

LOL, Diana responded. *Maybe she'll come back tonight.*

Sure. You'd like that but it's not exactly what I need.

Lily sat back and stared at the kitchen wall. What she really needed was a way—a decent way—to tell the ranch staff that the ranch would be sold and was probably closing. That and a good buyer.

A chime sounded from her phone, indicating a new text.

Gotta go, Diana wrote. *Lunch rush. Live long and prosper.*

Time diff is whipping my ass, Lily responded, realizing anew that in Florida it was two hours later. *Wrk smarter nt harder.*

Lily took her dishes to the sink and washed up as she planned her day. She needed to go into Morris and set up the realty listing. The sooner she got the process started, the less time she would need to spend in New Mexico and that was a good thing.

The woman from the night before haunted her thoughts. What kind of warped imagination was capable of creating such detail? It had to be a dream. Or the simple raving of her stressed-out mind. Sage said dreams delivered messages and Lily gave a lot of thought to what the messages could be. She knew about Los Alamos, about the scientific labs there. Was the message a subconscious memo that her father was involved with that somehow? Or with another woman? The strange woman said she was a colleague of her father's. Lily looked out the window as she dried her hands. Crazy. The whole thing was crazy. The ranch was too far from Los Alamos...

Lanny was standing in the barn doorway when Lily stepped off the front porch. Taking a deep breath and tucking her after-breakfast cigarette butt into her jeans pocket, she walked toward him. He seemed to ignore her approach, his gaze never wavering from his study of the ranch scrubland.

"I'm sorry," she said, looking up into his placid, averted face. "I...I don't know what else to do."

She turned and looked out across the wide expanse of front plain, her gaze following his. "I'm not blaming anyone. Mama doesn't want to come back here and...you know I used to...I love this place. It's not that... It's... She sighed heavily. "It's what I have to do."

She glanced up at him, willing him to look at her. He didn't.

"We each have our own path to follow," he said, his voice low and gravelly. "It's not for me to say."

"But will you still love me?" she asked, turning him and forcing him to regard her. "I couldn't bear..."

Her voice hitched and Lanny slowly drew her into his arms.

"Actions and love are not the same," he told her. "They exist in different worlds."

Lily allowed herself to weep openly then, held securely in his arms. She found herself weeping, oddly enough, for the loss of her father. Lanny held her a long time, as if understanding the tears.

Later, driving the ranch truck across the deserted, seemingly endless road into the town of Morris, Lily thought about Lanny's words. Though the words were reassuring, she wasn't one hundred percent sure that the close relationship she enjoyed with Sage and Lanny would continue. How could it? This was a betrayal, going against all that the Natives cherished. Land was not simply land to them. It was a commitment. It was a ritual joining of man and nature. Of the People and the Mother who sustains them. To give up that land to a stranger…well, it was a bigger loss than it appeared at first.

She sighed and set her mouth in a grim line. There was no other choice.

An abrupt feeling snatched at her and she glanced to her left and spied a woman standing alongside the side of State Route 23 just ahead. Lily slowed her speed and studied the woman as she passed her. She was older, in her seventh decade, with long gray hair braided and pulled forward in front of one shoulder. She was wearing a brown cardigan buttoned above a long dark blue skirt whose hem barely brushed the top of brown work boots. But it was her eyes that drew Lily's attention. Crystal blue and piercing, they seemed to lance across Lily like lasers. Their eyes met in a long, slow-motion moment and some type of communication happened. Lily was suddenly, oddly, comforted. She felt like she could breathe again and indeed, she drew in a deep, shuddering breath. Somehow she knew that everything would work out as it should.

She craned her neck to maintain contact, but it had been broken. The feeling of well-being lingered, though. Seconds later and there was no sign the woman had been there. Lily saw only tall greenery where she'd been standing.

The small town of Morris, New Mexico, had fallen into a siesta state this close to lunchtime. Passing Harper's Restaurant, which had been there on the main thoroughfare for decades, Lily saw tables full of diners behind the large, plate-glass front windows. The newer fast-food restaurants were filling up too, by the look of the crowded parking lots. Faded banners billowed around the Chevrolet dealership and Lily shook her head as she passed it by. Trucks. Lots of pickup trucks with a precious few commuter cars. She passed two gas stations and reflexively checked the gas gauge. Full. Of course. She spied Brookhouse Realty on the next block and pulled to the curb in front of the street-side business that was housed in an old, refurbished clapboard home.

As far as she knew, Bobby Brookhouse's business was the only realty concern in town. It was the only one she remembered, at any rate. She'd gone to elementary school with Lenny Brookhouse and knew he was considered very well off. Obviously, his father knew what he was doing.

Inside, Lily was greeted by a bespectacled older lady, someone she didn't recognize. Lily told her that she had a property to sell, and within ten minutes, she was sitting across from Mr. Robert F. Brookhouse himself. Much older than she remembered him, he eyed her with veiny, jaundiced eyes.

"So, Ducky Dawson's girl. I heard about your father. Tough luck that. Heart seems to get all of us sooner or later," he offered in a creaky, old man voice. "Especially the men."

"Yes, sir," Lily agreed, pulling down the sleeve of her light jacket to make sure the elf tattoo on her wrist was covered. She somehow knew he wouldn't approve.

"And you want to list the ranch?" His eyes lit perceptively. "All of it?"

"Yes, sir. My father left it to me, but Mama and I have a business down in Florida. I don't think we'll be moving back here."

Brookhouse pulled out a crisp new file folder and wrote *Dawson, Lily* neatly on the tab with a black marker. "What I'll do is send someone out to get photos of the estate, then we'll put it on our website as well as the national database. I'll pull the deed so we'll know the exact acreage and the original sale price."

Lily nodded. "Can you give me an estimate of when the listing might go live? I've only set aside two weeks to be here…"

Brookhouse nodded slowly. "I understand. We certainly can get it live before then and we can handle the sale for you if you're not here. We do that a lot with people who own multiple properties and want to move one. Nowadays everything can be done over the computer—I have some young people who handle all that."

He smiled at her, baring overlarge, yellowed teeth. The smile was made even more terrifying by the sun-speckled flesh of his scalp beneath his thinning hair. "I admit to being a dinosaur when it comes to technology," he added. "But I know there's ways to sign things legally by long distance. It shouldn't be a problem."

"Thank you," Lily murmured. Dinosaur was a good word for him, she decided.

"Now," he leaned and examined a datebook, "would tomorrow be a good day for my man to come photograph?"

Lily nodded and smiled. Looks like he wasn't going to drag his feet on this. "That would be fine. What time?"

"How about eight in the morning? Usually the light is good then."

Lily agreed and after a few more inane pleasantries, she stepped back onto Cross Street, Morris's main thoroughfare. She decided that she needed a drink. Yes, it was only midday but she desperately needed the bolster of alcohol. Hopping into the truck, she drove four miles through town until she came to the far side. Few things there had changed although she had to admit, certain aspects of the town were beginning to resemble old Western ghost towns.

But it was still there. Jake's Bar and Grill. The dilapidated wooden structure had been there long before Lily's birth and she was glad to see it was still going strong. It was a Morris landmark, offering good home cooking that her family had enjoyed often. Maybe not as snooty as some of the other historic buildings, but a landmark nonetheless.

The smoky interior was just as she remembered it, even down to the familiar, pickled rummies who were holding up the bar. There was, however, a different bartender. A woman, a red-haired woman, stood solidly behind the pocked but polished wooden bar. Lily took a seat at one end of the bar and studied the rail on the wall, trying to decide what she wanted. Something clear. Something cold. Something refreshing.

Suddenly the bartender appeared before her. She had a pale, freckled face and pale blue eyes that Lily would recognize anywhere.

"Oh, my fucking God, it *is* you," the woman said loudly, drawing the attention of everyone in the bar. "Lily Dawson, as I live and breathe."

"Heya, Tessie," Lily said, standing on the footrail so she could fling her arms around Tessie's neck. "Since when did you start working at Jake's?"

"Since I bought it, darlin'," she said, leaning on the gleaming bar and studying Lily with keen eyes. "You remember old Luke Winters, right? He used to tend bar here? Well, he started with the Alzheimer's so the owner, Roy, hired me to replace him. Well, Roy lives over in Nevada now and one day about two years ago he up and asks me if I want to buy the bar and hell..." She slammed a bottle of vodka on the bar. "I wasn't doing anything else so I said why not and here I go, owning Jake's Bar and Grill."

She measured two shots into old-fashioned glasses over ice and used the soda nozzle to top them off. She handed one to Lily and lifted hers in a toast.

"To old friends," she said.

"To old friends," Lily echoed.

CHAPTER EIGHT

"Are you sure you want to do that?" Tess asked Lily.

They were on their second vodka and were feeling no pain. Tess had ordered food for them, to temper the alcohol. She had also come around the bar to the customer side and now sat next to Lily, her left elbow on the bar, the hand supporting her head as she regarded her old friend. "Maybe you should just come back here. Morris ain't so bad. There's worse."

Lily thought of Florida. Yes, there was worse. "Mama doesn't want to. She likes it down there. She has her cronies in the trailer park and they get together every evening and drink and swap not-so-believable tales from their lives."

"So what do you do?" Tess lifted her glass and the ice resettled noisily.

"I waitress. It's okay." Lily shrugged.

"Would your mama do okay on her own?"

"Not really." Lily sighed and shifted on the barstool. "By eight every night, she's pretty well soused. I hang out and make sure everything's maintained."

Tess nodded. "I get that. You remember how my dad was, don't you?"

"I do."

"There's nothing you could say that would make her want to come here?"

"Nope. When I told her Ducky had left me the ranch she just gave me the lifted eyebrow."

Tess snickered into her drink. "Oh, no, not the lifted eyebrow!"

Lily laughed and scooted her drink to one side so the cook could set their food on the bar. Hand-cut french fries and stuffed mushrooms.

The cook, a handsome, athletic-looking high school boy, slung a dishtowel over his shoulder and winked at Lily. "Best in New Mexico," he said as he walked back to the kitchen.

Lily smiled at Tess. "Do you pay him to say that?"

Tess giggled and covered her mouth with both hands, resembling a two-year-old. A twenty-something, large-bodied two-year-old. She reached for a mushroom. "Try them. You'll see I don't have to," she replied, her mouth full.

Lily reached for a fry and tried it. Salty, hot, and plump. She nodded. "Hmm, he may be right."

"Okay, back to the ranch. You know, we had a lot of fun there. Remember swimming in that little pond at the end of Dillon's Run?"

"And how we came out to one another up in the barn?"

Tess frowned, but her eyes were sparkling with merriment. "Hey, how come you never tried anything with me?"

"Not my type. I like those itty-bitty dark butches with the short, short hair and sexy green eyes." Lily reached for another fry but swooped up a mushroom instead.

"Who has your heart these days?" Tess asked, growing serious. "I don't see anyone with you. It sure would be nice to have some moral support. Especially if you plan to sell."

Lily sighed. "It would, but I'm flying solo this trip. I was with someone back home, but she decided a new, younger model was a good thing for her."

"Ouch," Tess muttered.

"How about you? Is it slim pickings out here?"

"You mean a girlfriend? Nope, not now. I was with Laurie Mays for a bit. You remember her?"

"Umhm. What happened?" Lily asked, stuffing a new fry into her mouth.

"Her parents, well, her dad, got sick up in Idaho. She moved there to take care of them. Help her mom out."

"And you didn't like Idaho?" Lily studied Tess curiously.

"It wasn't me," Tess said, sighing then shaking up the ice in her glass. "Her parents said over their dead body. I mean, I own a *bar*."

Lily nodded knowingly. "Gotcha."

"Seriously. Don't you think you should reconsider? I mean, there's a lot of good memories out there," Tess offered.

"And some bad," Lily replied, draining her glass.

Tess nodded in understanding. "Another?"

"Nope, gotta scoot. Before I sell, I've got to decide what to do with all that crap out there. I'm gonna try to sell the furnishings and all, but my dad had some personal stuff that needs to be packed or tossed. You need anything? Office supplies? Furniture?"

Tess shook her head. "I can't get my head around it. No more Good Neighbor Ranch. Are you *sure*? It's only been five years you've been gone. You can manage the ranch okay."

"Nope, don't want to. And I have to be sure to be able to do it. The hardest thing is displacing everyone who works there. Sage and Lanny have been there since we moved from DC, like twenty years ago. I don't know what to do about that."

Tess poked an index finger at the ice in her glass. She looked morose and wistful. "Nothing *to* do. Change is the only constant."

Lily studied her. "You okay?"

"Yeah. It's just been really good to see you. I hate that you're going away again. I don't have too many friends here in town now that you're gone."

"Here. Let me give you my number. Do you have a smartphone?"

Tess wrestled one from her jeans pocket, fiddled with the keyboard then handed it to Lily.

Lily typed in her number, then called herself from Tess's phone so she would have Tess's number.

She studied Tess, feeling sad. She had missed her old friend.

"Well, I'm glad you're keeping this run-down old shed open. I'd hate to see it go away," she said cheerfully, trying to banish her sadness. She smiled at the laminated badge Tess wore pinned to her chest. It proclaimed, "No, I'm not Jake."

Tess reached out and touched her cheek in a gentle nudge. "Good to see you, hon. Stop back in before you leave town, okay?"

Lily stood and pulled out her wallet. "Sure will." She fished out a twenty and laid it on the bar. Tess snatched it up and stuck it down Lily's shirt. It was an old, familiar move from their childhood and Lily laughed out loud. Tess smiled at her beguilingly and Lily left the money in her shirt, knowing better than to try and pay, now. Instead, she moved close to Tess and pulled her into an embrace, the money crinkling loudly as it pressed between them. They stayed that way a long time.

Before leaving Morris, Lily stopped by Courthouse Square and went into the Taylor County Office of Records and Deeds. After hearing a half hour of local gossip from Nance Edwards who worked in the records office, Lily managed to make photocopies of her father's land surveys. She keenly remembered the purchase, even though she'd only been about six or seven years old. The announcement that her father had bought a ranch in New Mexico, sight unseen, had been shocking and inexplicable. And he hadn't even tried, really, to explain, simply assuming that they would leave their comfortable urban brownstone in central DC to take up ranching life in the New Mexico desert. And somehow they had.

She also remembered her parents' faces upon first seeing the ranch house. Her mother's face had expressed dismay and disappointment though she had tried to paste on a positive demeanor. Lily's father's face had been speculative. She knew, even at that young age, that the run-down ranch was a new challenge for him. Though she didn't know the particulars, she had a hunch that buying the ranch had something to do with his consulting work. Maybe he'd needed a quiet place for all the paperwork he worked on each evening. Or maybe, after leaving a full-time job at Bolling, he'd needed a new project to occupy him. She wasn't sure and her father never shared anything about his work or, for that matter, even his hobbies or passions. Conversations with General Ducky Dawson centered on current national affairs, practical matters, or occasionally her grades at school.

Lily's parents had begun the remodel of the newly dubbed Good Neighbor Ranch with enthusiasm. They'd drawn up plans and hired crews to come in and replace walls, install appliances, and lay new floors. Lily had gotten a big four-poster bed and had an active say in how her room was decorated. She'd gone with a cowboy theme to honor her new, exciting ranch life.

Though her mother had been enthusiastic at first, after a few years that enthusiasm had waned. By the time Lily was attending Morris Allied Junior High School, she would return home most days to find her mother so inebriated that she could barely stand. It had become a troubling secret that Lily had carried on her shoulders every day from that point onward. Her father had ignored it as long as he could, but then the daily battles had begun.

Lily tried to shake away the troubling memories as she headed back to Good Neighbor. She studied the scenery as she passed and realized that there was something soothing about the muted desert colors and the slanting play of light against the rocks. It seemed as though the sunlight actually painted the rocks with artistic abandon, shadowing certain areas, highlighting others. Once again, she found herself wishing she'd had artistic talent and could have captured the sun's inventive meanderings on her own canvas. Her talents had lain elsewhere, however. There had been no other career path for her, other than managing her mother's life and business, with a dollop of waitressing thrown in for good measure. Whether from nature or nurture, she had become good at organizing and controlling situations so that they didn't get out of hand.

CHAPTER NINE

The sprawling ranch house was deserted, but the pervasive smell of cleanser and lemon let her know that Sage had returned from the market and had been her usual tidy self. Lily strolled through the living room, gliding her fingertips lightly across the freshly cleaned surfaces. The surrounding desert was a sandy, dirty environment and daily dustings of the furniture were almost a necessity. The heavy drapes had been drawn against the harsh high-desert sun and the living room was cool and welcoming.

Her old room was on the northern end, separated from the kitchen by a small bathroom. She strode toward it, realizing that she hadn't been in it since arriving back in New Mexico. The door stuck a bit as she pushed it open and a draft of stale air peppered her. She stepped in and was suddenly twelve years old again, sitting morosely at the small, built-in desk in the corner, pondering her mother's habitual drinking. Nothing in the room had changed in the past five years, although Sage had made up the double bed and neatened the disarray Lily had left when she and her mother had departed. Lily keenly remembered her anger and despair at leaving the ranch. She wondered—had her father ever sat in this room, missing her?

Quickly she backtracked and pulled the door solidly closed. No need to dwell on the past.

Lily took in a deep breath and headed to her father's office on the western side of the house. She felt his presence keenly in there. The room was filled with framed awards and honors as well as framed certificates of higher learning. One wood-paneled wall was filled with framed photos of her father with various celebrities, air force men, and politicians. She moved close so she could study his face. Yep, it was Ducky. She touched the glass over his smiling eyes and felt a lurch of sorrow. Whatever he had been to her, he had been a successful, happy military man. That was something, right? He'd been one of the smartest people she'd ever met and she had always admired that about him. As well as his can-do attitude. And he never would have been described as lazy. His energy had seemed boundless, endless.

She sighed and let her hand drop. But his energy had finally ended.

Lily moved away from the wall of photos and passed behind her father's huge wooden desk. She sank slowly into his plush leather chair and pressed her palms against the top of the desk, moving the chair forward. She rested her chin in her cupped palms, her elbows propped on the desk surface as she pondered where to begin the packing up. She glanced at the books weighing down the bookshelves and felt anxiety fill her. How could she hope to get all this done in two weeks? Calming herself, she reached for her father's notepad and pen, arranged neatly next to the posed family portrait sitting on the polished desktop, and began to make a list. She needed help with the packing and listed Sage, Margie, and Eddie Molinero's wife, Cathy. If the four of them worked long days, they could probably sort through the items that had made up her father's life by the end of two weeks. The heavy lifting could be done by the farmhands and they could also transport items to the donation centers and arrange for the shipping of anything she wanted to keep. Looking around the office, she quickly decided that there would be precious little of that.

Fishing her cell phone from her pocket, she activated it and pressed the camera icon. There was no need to take all this crap with her. Photos would suffice. She rose and slowly walked around the room, photographing the framed certificates, the photos of her father with famous people, and then a few overviews of the room from each direction. Her attention was drawn to the tall glass sculpture that rested on the right side of her father's desk. It had a twin on the mantel in his bedroom and she wondered why he'd needed two of them. She squared it in her viewfinder on the back of her phone. It was pretty, with smooth, flowing curves of glass, maybe even crystal, which caught light and moved it in wonderful ways. She pressed the shutter button and checked the picture, smiling at the slight rainbow of light she'd captured in its depths. Maybe she would take one of them with her, although where she'd put it in her small trailer bedroom would be a problem.

Reseating herself at the desk, she opened the drawers, searching for any important paperwork that needed to be kept. There wasn't much because her father had kept his most important documents with his lawyer and copies of those papers were in a FedEx box back in her bedroom in Florida.

In the center drawer, amidst an unruly tangle of office supplies and colorful pens, lay a leather-bound, eight-by-ten iPad. No, it was an Android tablet. She tapped it awake and saw a field for a password. She grunted. Well, that would be almost impossible to decipher, but it would be nice to have her own tablet. Maybe she could have it reset to the factory settings. She placed it to one side, along with its charger, and set about investigating the other desk drawers. There was nothing of import, mostly office supply materials and a few computer printouts that looked like Greek to her. She found a bundle of letters that she had sent to her father during a short period of time after the divorce and the move to Florida. She set those aside, with the tablet. Why not keep them? It was a part of her history, after all. It might be a good, necessary thing to relive, at some point, the feelings of loss she had felt before bitterness had set in.

There was little else in the desk. She saw a few weird books on physics, a book by Carl Sagan about the cosmos, and several guidebooks from the air force. She leafed through some of them and decided they weren't worth much of her time or her energy.

Closing the final drawer with a satisfying slam, Lily rose and stretched. She moved to the window and pulled aside the heavy drapery. Evening had crept up on her and she could smell the scent of Sage's good food wafting from the kitchen. She felt a sense of relief that it was dinnertime. Being alone for so long in her father's study had become a little creepy. She gathered up the tablet, the letters, and a few of the other papers and carried them out of the office and down the hall to her father's bedroom.

Lanny, Margie, and Sage were standing in the kitchen when she came back down the hall. Margie waved the bottom of an iced tea glass imperiously at Lily.

"Is it true? What they say? You're going to sell?"

Lily gave Lanny a pained expression before sighing loudly. "Yes, I think I have to, Margie. I...I'm not a rancher."

"What does your ma say about this?" Margie interrupted loudly.

Lily sank into a chair at the table. "She wants me to, Margie. Insisted on it."

Margie stood in silence a long beat. "Well, what do *you* want to do?" she asked finally.

Lily covered her face with both hands. "I don't know, Margie. I just don't know any more."

"Well, you'd better know. A lot of lives depend on what you decide."

Lily looked up at her, anger festering. "You really think I don't *know* that? But what do you expect me to do, abandon Mama and move here? Or force her back to the place she detests more than any other place? I don't seem to have any good choices, now do I?"

"Where is your ma? Why didn't she come with you?"

Lily frowned. "I just told you, Margie. She wants no part of this place."

Margie wriggled in frustration, one hand tapping against her large, soft belly. She looked to Sage hopefully. "Maybe if we all pool our savings, we can buy it ourselves. And keep it running."

Sage shook her head. "You have savings?"

Margie looked hard at each of their faces and then slammed the glass of tea onto the counter. "Fuck this!" she said as she pushed through the kitchen door.

Sage, Lanny, and Lily stared in silence at the creaking screen door.

"Well, that went well," Lily muttered.

"No one promised it would be easy, I suppose," Sage said as she brought a bowl of mashed potatoes to the table. "Sit down, both of you, and eat. We'll let time handle this one," she added.

"Time. Now that's something I don't have a lot of," Lily replied, as she reached for the platter of fried chicken.

"A long time ago, before my father's father," Lanny began in his low, resonant voice. "The Spanish came to our city. The People gave them food. Gave them water, but they stole from our stores of grain." He laid a biscuit reverently on his plate.

"When we tried to take the grain back, soldiers died. More soldiers came and though we fought with bravery, in the cold and snow, they captured men, women, and children and destroyed Sky Village."

Sage's head was bowed in respect as she listened to the tale unfold.

"They took who was left, leaving thousands dead, and the People had to walk from our home. They enslaved our boys and women and maimed our men. But some of us escaped and made our way back to Sky Village and we rebuilt better than before." He turned to make sure Lily was watching. "I think we will survive," he said gently.

Sage laid one hand over Lily's, drawing her attention. "Margie is not one of us," she said, as if in explanation.

Lanny and Sage began to eat as Lily sat dumbfounded. Somehow she had won the Kya'nahs' approval. She twirled her fork in her mashed potatoes, her thoughts conjuring the tragic images from history that Lanny's words had evoked.

CHAPTER TEN

"Are you doing any better, Mama?"

There was only one lamp on in the bedroom, and Lily had been enjoying the spotlighted solitude, which had left her to her thoughts and dismal plans. She knew she had to check on her mother though, to find out if she was okay.

"I think so," Sandy replied, with a short cough. "Lucy brought me some medicine and they've kept me in bed all day long. I'd better be getting better."

Lily breathed a sigh of relief. "Well, good. I'm very glad to hear that. I was worried. You don't get sick too often."

Sandy laughed. "Yeah, must be some kind of freak coincidence. Lots of people down here have the flu, though, so it's no real surprise."

She coughed long and loudly. "So tell me, what's happening out there in the land of enchantment?" Her voice, though raspy, still managed to ring teasingly.

Lily pondered how much she should tell her mother. "It's okay, Mama, but...well, I'm catching some flack about selling. Margie was here and was fit to be tied when she found out."

"Figures," Sandy replied sourly.

"Mama, she was your friend," Lily chastised.

"Yeah, and I needed a friend back then. You don't see her carting her black ass down here to see me, do you?"

"Mama, don't be shitty," Lily warned.

"Yeah, yeah," Sandy replied feebly. "It's not like any of those so-called friends in DC came out to New Mexico, either," she added ruefully.

"I know, Mama, and I'm sorry."

They had played briefly with the idea of returning to DC, but offers of help or support with resettling had been slow in coming and, angered anew, Sandy had leapt on the management opportunity in Florida.

"It'll be okay, Mama. We'll get through it somehow." She wondered suddenly who the "we" was that she was talking about.

"Just hang tough, sweetheart. You can do this."

"I will, Mama. You just keep getting better, okay?"

They signed off and she lay back against the pillows, placing her phone on the nightstand. The peace and quiet of the room stole across her and she felt optimistic. She could and would do this thing.

The lopsided stack of papers across the room drew her eye, and she rose and fished out her father's tablet from the stack. She carried it and the charger back to the nightstand and plugged it into the power strip there. The screen lit immediately and Lily saw the expected bolt of lightning in the upper right corner that told her the machine was charging. She studied the password field curiously. What would her father have chosen?

Shrugging, she pressed the keyboard icon and typed in *Lily*. A big black window appeared with a Samsung warning across the top. It informed her that she had used up one of her password tries and that she had nine more before the memory on the tablet would be wiped and it would return to factory mode.

"Wow," Lily muttered. "This is cool."

She didn't much care if it was reset, it was going to be hers now anyway, but it was fun trying to guess her father's password.

She exed out the warning and typed in *Sandy*.

The warning appeared again.

She paused in thought, not able to imagine what else his password could be.

She exed out the warning and typed in *air force*.

The warning reappeared. She was down to seven more tries. She pressed her bottom lip. What else did her father have in his life? Ah, the much-loved dog he'd had when he was a boy. She typed in *Canyon*. No luck.

After a few moments of thought, she typed in *Katherine*, her paternal grandmother's name. Again, no luck.

She set the tablet aside and rose from the bed. She entered the bathroom, used the toilet then brushed her teeth. Back in the bedroom, she pulled boxers and a tank top from the bureau and changed. She idly wondered what Sage had done with her father's civilian clothing as she folded the clothes she had shed and laid them across the hamper in the bathroom. Probably taken them up to the village to let her sons have them. Lily hoped so. She'd like to see them put to good use.

Ready for bed, she stood in the bedroom and stared belligerently at the tablet. It was driving home yet again how little she really knew her father. He'd been like a closed book, a mystery that she'd had to unravel every time she'd talked to him.

"Damn you, Daddy," she whispered angrily. "Why did everything have to be so fucking hard with you?" She looked around the room, noting anew how nondescript, how unlived in, it was. There was more of her mother's influence in these rooms, even five years after she'd left than there was of her father's. How strange was that? His one addition, the glass sculpture, winked at her from the mantel.

She sat on the bed and retrieved the tablet. She brightened the screen and glared at it. She abruptly dropped the cover closed and set it on the nightstand as she reclined against the pillows, chin on her chest. She thought of Ducky Dawson, trying to cement into her mind some of the good times before she would allow the memory of him to fade away for good. Images came to her. Once when Lily and her mother were at Lafayette Park, he had appeared unexpectedly, wearing his dress blues. He'd been so incredibly handsome and heroic to her five-year-old eyes.

She remembered sitting in his lap as he was reading thick reports marked urgent or confidential. She remembered early trips to the Washington Zoo and the National Aquarium, holding his hand as he talked intelligently about the displays. She remembered the first time he had sheepishly donned a cowboy hat. The time he'd bought one for Lily. The time they'd ridden a horse together. Closing her eyes, she tried to feel him, smell him, and found she could but only in brief snatches of sensation. Suddenly, she heard his voice in her head and saw his smiling eyes as they studied her.

Eyes snapping open, she sat upright and reached for the tablet. Awakening it, she typed in *LittleLil*. As if she had waved a magic wand, the home screen appeared. Lily smiled at her success. Studying the home screen, she saw that there was only one icon. It was titled *DDawsonJournal*.

Lily took a deep breath, her hands tightening about the tablet. Did she dare? Did she really want to know her father this intimately? And most importantly, would he disappoint her again?

Quickly, she closed the tablet and placed it back on the nightstand. She snapped off the light and slid beneath the blanket. She rested curled on her right side, the thin line of light from beneath the tablet cover mesmerizing her. No, it was not the right time. He'd only been dead six weeks. Not time enough.

She forced her eyes closed and tried to calm her leaping thoughts. The image of her father's deep blue eyes smiling at her kept reappearing in her mind's eye. She turned her back to the now darkened tablet, tucking the blankets more securely about her shoulders. Sudden tears burned in her eyes and she realized that he had left that journal *for* her. He wanted her to read it. Could she be that brave—to read the intricate details of his life?

He was brave. He'd won medals for his bravery during helicopter extractions in the Vietnam War. She'd seen the bright, thick ribbons on his dress uniform and heard the stories about the jungle.

She sat and flung the covers away and reached for the light. The leather-covered tablet was still waiting. Waiting for her. She opened it, reawakened it, and retyped the password. After taking a deep breath, she poked the folder with an index finger. A new window opened with nine empty blocks and a hint at the bottom. SS. SS? Lily slowly blinked her eyes, disappointment paralyzing her. She had worked herself up to finally read her father's journal and then hit this new barrier. Her eyes lifted and she stared unseeingly at the opposite wall, her mind whirring. SS. Secret service? Nazi youth guard? Nine empty blocks. What did it mean?

Her eyes dropped to the tablet. Nine…numbers? Social security? That had to be it. New excitement filled her but was extinguished just as quickly. She didn't know her father's social security number. She thought of the papers in the mailing box back in Florida. She had seen the numbers there, but no matter how hard she tried to focus, they would not appear clearly in her mind. Maybe the numbers were in his office. She shifted on the bed, feet hitting the floor as she debated whether to wait until morning to look for it.

Time stood still for a short time as she sat in indecision. A sudden thought intruded and she studied the tablet. Warily, slowly, not sure what would happen should she be wrong, Lily typed in her own social security number. With a cheerful chime the tablet brightened and an enormously long list of image and text documents appeared. She scrolled down and saw they covered all the months—years—since Lily and her family had moved to the ranch. Hesitantly, she clicked on the first one. It was a scanned PDF image, obviously made from a paper journal and inserted.

Journal Entry
March 3, 1998
General Lurashi at BOSA has finally passed the gauntlet after three weeks of deliberation. I think he really wanted to be the liaison, as this issue probably does fall under his purview of outer space affairs.

I should note how humbled I am to have been the one chosen by the IDB collective. My first midnight meeting with the representative IDB was congenial and after my initial fright eased, I found it to be intelligent and forthcoming. This manifestation of them, whom I call Flynn because its name is unpronounceable, will be my regular contact. It is one of them who has an interest in our well-being, although I don't understand all the particulars. I often feel a sense of wait and see resonating from it. I hope that with time and patience, it will understand that I, too, believe in the partnership of our world and their dimension. That I understand and appreciate the incredible gifts the IDBs give to the people of earth, time and again.

I agonize daily about taking this new position, accepting this honor of being chosen. I wish a sparser population wasn't so important for the IDBs although I recognize how powerful their energy can be, very noticeable in a crowd of people.

Carrying this burden alone is hard. I wish I could explain this new work to San and why moving west is so necessary. She doesn't comprehend the importance of what I am doing. I didn't even tell her about the promotion and pay increase, knowing how she would react, how she would rail that more duties will mean even less time with her and with my precious Lily.

As if it wasn't all for them.

As if I weren't trying to preserve the world status quo for them, to make their world a safe and blissfully ignorant, blank slate.

Telling San the whole truth is not allowed anyway, so it's a moot point whether she could understand the importance of what I will do. To her I'm just an administrator, a pencil pusher at the beck and call of an unfeeling government.

The extra funds will make the transition to Outpost Good Neighbor easier for all concerned, and the BOSA agency is buying my DC house, which also helps. Yet, I truly hate uprooting all of us. San was so angry, so afraid—but she is, and always has been, a good military wife. Isolating her is secondary to the position but she is so wrapped up with her friends, her charities here in DC... And Little Lil. What about the schools and other kids in New Mexico? I have no answers but trust our government to lay the pathways out for me. The greater good, I tell myself often...

I think about the guys at the club, men I have served with, got drunk with. It's almost as if they—or I—have died in battle.

This will be a lonely life.

The greater good, I tell myself.

Then I think about the bomb. The one the Al-Qaeda radicals planted in the basement of the White House. I think about what might have happened had the IDBs not warned us. And the time the Greys took control of Secretary Maxwell and tried to incite a war. I think of the raids on the Nevada compound that require the IDBs' constant presence...

Interrupted by San. She is crying again...What can I do? Telling her that she—all of us—is surrounded by an unseen population... several of them...well, it's disturbing. And to prove it would be to go against years of security training. It would destroy my career. And destroy my family's peace of mind.

No, I take the brunt of this storm.

Lily tore her eyes from the tablet and stared wide-eyed at the wall. A shiver coursed along her spine and she had to bite her bottom lip to keep from crying out. IDBs? What insanity had her father become involved with?

She thought back and found that she remembered her father working on this very tablet. At the time, she hadn't paid much attention, assuming he was handling more work-related paperwork. Tears swelled in her eyes and she swallowed slowly.

IDBs...what did that mean? Although filled with insatiable curiosity, Lily knew that walking this new journey alongside her father was too powerful, the emotions too strong. She closed the tablet and placed it on the nightstand. Her mind was whirling and she reclined and closed her eyes. She thought of the Roswell crash. She thought of the dozens of yearly UFO sightings in New Mexico. Was this why they had been uprooted and moved west to the ranch? To allow her father to monitor UFOs? Or UFO sightings? Crazy. She wasn't even sure she believed in them. In the past, though the idea of it was intriguing, she had always scoffed at true believers.

"Stop," she told herself aloud.

Sleep, she needed to sleep. It was late and she would be able to deal with this tomorrow with a clear, fresh mind. She opened her eyes and reached out to touch the closed tablet once more, the connection to her father palpable. She pulled the hand back and turned on her side, bringing her knees up until she was in a fetal position. She wrapped her arms about her shoulders, refusing to see her father's kind eyes, even though they kept appearing in her imagination. She forced her eyes closed and forced herself to focus on nothing.

CHAPTER ELEVEN

"Lily. Lily, you need to wake up now." The voice was gentle, soothing, but urgent.

Lily frowned in her sleep. There was something troubling her, but it was too soon to remember it.

"Please, Lily. It's important."

Lily opened one eye and realized she'd fallen asleep with the bedside lamp on. "Saysay?"

"Lily?"

A face appeared before her, and a rough, core-shaking buzz rode through her. The face had silver eyes and was surrounded by cropped white hair.

Lily cried out and sat up, her heels sinking into the mattress and propelling her back, toward the headboard. Thus protectively ensconced, she stared at the woman who had been in her previous dream. She moaned.

"Oh, my God, you're real," she choked out.

The woman, who had reared back to her full diminutive height, wrapped her arms about herself and studied Lily.

"We assumed you knew that," she said.

Lily shook her head. "No. No! I thought I'd dreamed you, of course."

Flynn nodded reasonably. "Of course."

She began to pace as Lily's wide eyes followed her. "Please hear us now. There is a new threat..."

"Threat?" Lily interrupted.

Flynn paused and eyed Lily. "Your father...worked...have you learned about your father's work with us?"

Lily sighed loudly. "I think so. He—he kept a journal. I read a little bit of it. You're an alien, right?"

Lily couldn't even believe the words coming from her own mouth. To her surprise, Flynn shook her head in the negative.

"No, not...but... It depends on...definition. I am not of your world but I am also not from this or any other galaxy... world."

"But..." Lily frowned at her then took a deep breath to organize and calm her thoughts. "Okay. Tell me what an IDB is."

"InterDimensional Being. This name is for humans to perceive what we are. We exist as an energy...collective that splintered off from your present dimension in the...time before your memory. We exist in all dimensions and also between them."

"Wait, how can that be?" Lily interjected. "I don't understand. You're standing here."

"Yes," Flynn agreed, nodding slowly. "But we are energy in its...purest form, the inception of your...atom. We use ambient matter to take this form as it is one you understand."

"So you can be anything?" Lily was trying to wrap her mind around this concept.

"Yes, but there is no time...now. We have contacted your leaders many times from...millennia...ago. Once when there was a...death...from a breathing illness. Many of your people died but we...helped...so not all died."

Lily took this in slowly. "Was that...wait, was that back in 1918? During that flu that killed, like, fifty million people?"

Flynn tilted her head as if pondering the question. Silence cloaked them for almost a full minute. "We do believe that is… truth. Time is hard for us but…your history…documents… prove it so."

Lily nodded. "So—all this time. All this time, you've been what? Helping Earth? How can a being of energy have such compassion?"

Flynn appeared surprised but took the time to respond thoughtfully. "What is this…compassion but energy focused? Do you think of energy as cold…unfeeling?"

"Well, yes, I suppose," Lily responded, frowning in thought.

"This is…false. We are the warmth of energy and energy can become anything. Even …compassionate."

"Ahh," Lily muttered, trying to understand.

"We must track…time now. Once again there are… destructive entities. From another place…planet… You call them Greys. They seek to…to harm your people and take your…land."

"Why do they want our land?"

Flynn brushed Lily's comments aside as she began pacing again. She paused for several seconds. "You call them…minerals. They need your world's minerals."

"That makes sense," Lily answered thoughtfully. "Are they a threat now, still?"

"Yes." Flynn stood still before Lily. "We need your leader's permission to…save the water. Greys have harmed it."

Alarm flashed in Lily and she rose, facing Flynn. "Harmed it? How?"

Flynn backed away almost immediately as strong energy buzzed through Lily again, making her knees bend. She almost fell but the edge of the bed caught her.

"Again…you must not get too…close in this form of flesss …flesh," Flynn murmured. "It could harm your…heart."

Lily's thoughts tumbled over themselves. "Heart? Wait— did you harm my father?"

Flynn recoiled, her face filled with surprise. "Never. We could never harm…any of you. It is not our way."

"What about accidentally?" Lily persisted. "Did you get too close to him?"

"No, we would not. Not without warning him away."

Lily squinted at her, anger a familiar emotion, much better than the rioting emotions threatening her from these new revelations. "How can you be sure? Maybe it was another one. Someone else in your…collective."

Flynn smiled and it was oddly endearing to Lily. "We are one," she said simply. "We would all know of this."

Sighing, Lily lowered herself and sat on the bed. "Okay. Tell me about the water."

A small chair suddenly shimmered into being behind Flynn and she sat down. Lily's eyes grew wider.

"There is a smaller…alien form…you call it virus…that is in the water now. Many are already ill from this. Many will die as…blood…thickens. We cannot save all but if your leader will…allow, we will treat the water with…mineral salt silver. It has been…engineered to kill this entity only. It will not harm man or his…foodstuff."

Lily buried her face in her hands. She remained that way a very long time, part of her hoping that the IDB would be gone when she finally raised her head. It was a futile hope. Flynn was still there, waiting patiently and placidly watching her. "So, I'm guessing that you would tell this to my father and he would contact the powers that be," she said, knowing that this was the only plausible possibility. This whole scenario hit too close to home not to have been real.

Flynn nodded. "Yes. And we must…hurry. Many have taken the water and are…reacting to the alien. They are…dying."

Shit, Lily thought angrily. Yet one more insane thing that she had to deal with. "How do I know you aren't lying to me, making this up?"

Flynn swiveled and one hand lifted to the large, flat television on the wall above the fireplace. The screen brightened immediately to a headline news station. Lily and Flynn waited through the end of local weather and watched as breaking news returned.

"This illness, which many have dubbed the Polar Purge, has, at last count, caused the hospitalization of more than three hundred people in the Southwest. Sixty people have already died, but the CDC warns that this is an unconfirmed number and that, indeed, there could be many more."

The scene switched from the news desk to a remote interview in a busy hospital hallway. A harried physician, labeled as Doctor Timothy Alfred, was speaking.

"Yes, sure, I think that there are cases that have been unreported. This stuff is bad and I'm sure many are dying in their homes, thinking they have garden-variety stomach flu and not seeking out help."

The news anchor, a tired-looking older gentleman, returned abruptly.

"According to national labor statistics, work attendance in the Southwest is already at an all-time low as many employees risk losing their jobs rather than contracting the possibly deadly strain of flu. This is further encouraged by CDC and WHO warnings for Americans in the area to stay at home as much as possible, to not use public bathroom facilities, and to wash their hands several times each day. Back to Steve Innes, who is in Atlanta at the main offices of the CDC..."

Flynn waved a hand and the television went dark and silent.

"We must be...quick...to help as many as possible. Many are already infected and will die. We will save many, if we are fast."

Lily stared at Flynn, whose features blurred as her eyes filled with tears. "I don't want to do this, Flynn. Isn't there anyone else you can contact?"

Flynn watched Lily with sorrow manifesting in her strange, chrome eyes. "We are bound to only one contact by your leaders. We are not allowed to contact your director, only his... representative, our liaison."

Lily scrubbed at her eyes and stifled a sob. "Bastards don't want anyone else to know about you. Our government has more secrets than there are sands in the desert."

Flynn appeared to be confused by this reference but before she could contact her collective, Lily spoke on. "What is it you need me to do? Specifically."

"We need…permission…to add our cure to the water here. We have vowed to seek permission from…the government… for any change to this continent. Our…people…are in place and are ready to treat the water supply. You must seek this permission for us."

"So, me. I need to contact the president of the United States and ask him if you and your collective can put medicine in the water supply. Do you even understand how crazy this is? First of all, I can't even get close to him. Second, why would he even believe me?" A feeling of helplessness, powerlessness, swamped her.

"There is another," Flynn said thoughtfully, her head tilted to one side. "The name is Collins."

Lily straightened happily. "Of course, Uncally! He would know about you."

Flynn lurched in alarm. "No, he does not know of us. He is a…blind contact, your father said."

Lily thought a moment. Her godfather, Colonel Alan Collins, was her father's best friend. The two had met while in military school and had become close. He would know something.

"You must contact him and he will…guide you," Flynn added.

Lily looked at the clock and saw it was almost four in the morning here, six there. She needed to call him. They had talked briefly after her father's death but had not connected since. She wondered how he would react to this news. News. Was it really true? Her eyes found Flynn and she studied the being for some time. Suppose Flynn had created the television news footage in order to lie to her. She frowned. But to what end?

Lily sighed deeply. She was still having a hard time believing that the IDBs really existed.

"I'll call him," she said, filled with resignation. Living with the Natives for a good part of her life, she had learned that there was more than could be seen in the mere physical world that surrounded her. "Let me make sure I got this straight. You, your people, the InterDimensional Beings, need permission to treat the American drinking water to kill a virus. A virus put in the water by bad aliens to eventually kill the people of the US so that those aliens can mine the planet. Is that what I need to tell Uncally?"

Flynn placed her pale hands on her knees, the fingers drumming impatiently. "No, you must not tell him this. There is a…pass code, a password that will…enable you to see the leader. You must tell Collins the password only. He will arrange for you to see the leader. You must only tell the leader everything we have told you."

Lily's mouth fell open. "A password. I don't have a password. How can I have the password? My father never even mentioned *you* to me. Why would I have a password?" Her voice had risen as she was overtaken by panic.

Flynn's face grew sad and darkened. "I am sorry…Lily. I am very sorry."

Lily closed her eyes. The journal. Maybe the password was in the journal. But where? There had been years of entries in that folder. There was no way she could read them in time. She would have to call Collins and hope for the best. She started in surprise when Flynn's entire form flickered suddenly.

"How can I contact you?" Lily said quickly. "After I talk to him."

Flynn nodded and a gentle smile curved her sparkling, disintegrating lips. "We move in glass. Press your hand…entire hand…to any glass and I will…hear…you."

"Glass?" Lily asked curiously. "What kind of glass?"

Flynn frowned as if confused. "Kind? Glass. Just glass." She flickered again. "I am called…to…Lauderdale. A place called Lauderdale." She raised questioning eyes. "Do you know of this place?"

Lily shrugged. "Florida? There's a Fort Lauderdale, Florida."

"Hurry, Lily. Much depends on you. This will spread across the earth…and all will…will die."

A huge geyser of heat washed across Lily and she was inundated with the smell of burning hair as the fine hair on her forearms singed. She raised her arms to shield her face but the heat passed quickly.

CHAPTER TWELVE

Lily did not go back to sleep. She stared at the wall opposite her bed, awaiting the first stirring of daylight so she could call Collins. She had pondered the ramifications of what Flynn had told her. How could this be happening? She wished she could unhear it. If what Flynn said were true, then so many things had changed in her very psyche. Aliens were real. Other dimensions were real. The ending of life on Earth was—could be—real. What was she supposed to do with this? A big, huge part of her wanted to curl up under the covers and stick her thumb in her mouth, to wait for the Apocalypse to occur. Dying peacefully in bed seemed so…welcoming.

Then she lifted her eyes and stared at the ill, suffering victims on the local television news channel. She'd turned the TV back on after Flynn left and she'd been watching it periodically, without sound, for the past half hour.

It was called the Polar Purge, named for the coldness of the extremities in the infected. The death toll, from vomiting and diarrhea leading to a fatal dehydration plus strokes, had climbed.

It was now six thousand reported. Lily sighed and reached for her phone. It rang three times before Alan picked up.

"Lily? How are you?" he asked.

"There's a password I need to give you," Lily said without preamble. "I don't know it but my father used it to contact the mucky mucks in DC."

Alan took a deep breath. "Okay. Tell me your exact birthdate."

Lily complied in a quiet voice.

"What was the name of the first pet you had?"

Lily pulled on her bottom lip, trying to remember. She didn't remember because she'd been only one year old, but she'd seen photographs of the bedraggled, fuzzy-brown kitten. "Ewok. Mom named him—the cat—Ewok."

"That's it, you're in. Tell me what you need."

She could hear the relieved smile in his voice. "Oh, Uncally," she muttered sadly.

"I wondered if you knew of your dad's work," Alan said. His voice was a low whisper.

"I don't really know anything. I was just…contacted. How much do you know?"

"Nothing. I'm only a cleared connection to DC. Who do you need me to get in touch with?"

Lily's eyes widened and she sat up straighter. She took in a deep breath. "The president."

"Okay, the usual. He's new, though. Stay by your phone. I'll make the travel arrangements. It'll be a private jet at Sunport so be ready."

"Wait! I…I'm not going there…I have to. I can send the journal—"

"You have to go, hon. It has to be a face-to-face. I'm sorry."

She could hear his regret and wondered anew what she had gotten herself into. She thought of her mother and how confused and then incensed she'd be knowing Lily was flying to DC. She couldn't tell her about it. A sudden cold chill paralyzed Lily. Her mother had the flu. She moaned aloud.

"Lily? Lil? What's wrong? Are you okay? Lily, talk to me, damnit!!"

Lily swallowed hard and tried to even her breathing. "Yes, I'll be there. You tell me when."

"I've already put the call in while we were talking. It shouldn't be more than two hours muster time, then a few hours travel for you. Pack for a couple days, just in case."

"Yes, Uncally," Lily responded quietly. "I…miss you, love you. Take care of yourself and stay away from…from water, okay?"

"I know, honey. I have been. You too."

The phone beeped and Lily dropped her hand and looked down at the cell. She was fucking going to DC. Stirring herself, she leapt from the bed and hurried to shower and dress. Bathed, her hair dry, she stood in front of her open closet and bemoaned the lack of choices. What did one wear to meet the president of the United States? She sighed and took down the only nice blouse she'd brought on this trip. This blouse and her best jeans would have to do.

Down the hall, the kitchen was still dark, but Sage was at the counter, scrambling eggs in a glass bowl.

"What are you doing up so early," she asked, glancing at Lily, her perusal pausing when she noticed that Lily was fully dressed.

"Listen, I can't explain, but I have to go away for a few days. I'll be back but it's something I have to do."

"Well," Sage said, turning back to the counter. "Let me get you fed. I suppose you need a ride to the airport?"

Lily blinked slowly, feeling as though she had stepped into a stage play and hadn't even seen a script. "Yyy…yes, I do, in a couple hours."

Sage nodded and placed bacon onto a baking sheet. "Give me fifteen minutes to get some food ready, then I'll tell Lanny to take you."

"Can I help you?" Lily asked shyly. Her heart was beating hard in her chest, and she felt close to tears for some inexplicable reason.

"No, sweetness. I'm sure you have other things to do. Thank you for the offer though."

Lily looked up and saw the love and fondness shining deep in Sage's eyes. She smiled tremulously and reached to hold the older woman's hand. "Thank you for always being here," she said.

"Always," Sage responded, squeezing Lily's hand. "Always."

Lily strode through the front hall and out onto the front porch. She lit a cigarette and fished her cell from her pocket and called her mother. The phone rang, but there was no answer. She heard her mother's familiar phone message and tears filled her eyes. "Mom, listen. Call me as soon as you get this, okay? It's important."

One of the house's front windows snagged her gaze. She walked over to it and traced an index finger over the glossy surface. Any glass, Flynn had said. You can call us on any glass. What did that mean?

She touched the heavily painted wood encasing the glass then drew her hand away. She dialed the main office of the trailer park, knowing her mother would answer. She was keenly disappointed. George answered.

"George, hi, it's Lily. Is Mom okay? She's not answering her phone…"

"We sent her to the hospital, Lily. She had a relapse during the night and even had some trouble breathing." He coughed loudly and Lily heard him moan, as though coughing hurt.

"You're sick too?" she asked quickly.

"Oh, yeah. Everyone's got it. Raced through this place like wildfire." He laughed shortly. "I'm getting a little concerned. Half the park's in the hospital with it."

"Some stomach flu, huh?" Lily responded hollowly. A sharp pang of pain hit her in the chest. No, these were her friends and family…they couldn't…they wouldn't. She needed to go to her mother.

She gripped the phone tightly and straightened her shoulders. No. She needed to get her ass to DC.

"George, listen. I'll get there as soon as I can. Tell…please tell Mama that I love her. Will you do that for me?"

George coughed but tried to squelch it. "Of course, Lily. You don't need to be here. We don't want you getting this flu too. Stay healthy."

Lily was chilled to the bone. Yes, she too could catch this Polar Purge. She could die.

A sudden sound behind her drew her eyes to the drive. A plume of dust heralded the approach of a long, black sedan. Lily's mouth fell open. Was it...yes, it was turning onto the house's gravel drive. Lily sighed. She knew these types of cars. Government. She signed off with George and waited. Maybe they were coming here to take her to the plane.

The driver hurried from the car and opened the back door. Two men stepped into the brightening New Mexico morning. The first man, dressed in the full dress blue uniform cast a measuring gaze across the house, finally settling on Lily. He looked away and to the other man, obviously his aide, who handed him a fat folder. The two approached the porch.

"Good morning, gentlemen. What can we do for you?" She tried to look welcoming but there was something about the major that set her on edge.

The major removed his sunglasses before speaking. "Good morning, ma'am. We're here to see Miss Lilianne Dawson."

Lily sighed again. "That would be me. What is this about?" She wanted to add a query about the flu but had a hunch that giving this guy any information would not be a good thing.

"May we come in?" He smiled a false smile that she was sure had been practiced to the nth degree. She studied the major. He was middle-aged, probably late fifties, with cold blue eyes under bushy brows. His lips and cheeks looked weathered, but his military-issue teeth were large, white and perfect. He removed his cap, revealing a thick graying mat of short, blondish hair.

Lily reached to open the door and let the two men inside. "I have to tell you—this will be a short meeting. I have some urgent business to take care of."

The major's eyes drifted to the small overnight case and pocketbook she'd left by the door. "This shouldn't take too long."

Sage approached them along the hallway.

"Good morning. Would you like coffee?" she said.

The aide piped up suddenly, running a very practiced interference. "No, ma'am, thank you just the same."

Sage's gaze flicked to Lily but she turned and moved back toward the kitchen.

"Come this way, gentlemen. We can talk in the living room." She led them into the large spacious front room of the house. Sage had already opened the drapes and the view of the shadowed desert was spectacular, lit by the slow sunrise.

Lily sank into her father's usual chair and beckoned for the men to sit on the long sofa. They complied and the major cleared his throat before placing his cap and sunglasses down on the coffee table and running a hand over his tightly curled hair.

"First of all, let me introduce myself. My name is Major Leon Nilsson. I was a colleague, a friend, of your father. Let me say how sorry I am, miss, well, how sorry we all are, for your loss. He will be missed by all of us."

"Thank you," Lily responded automatically. She was watching the major warily. This couldn't be good.

"I'm Airman First Class Anthony Cohen, ma'am. Nice to meet you." The aide introduced himself and held out his hand. Lily took it and smiled at the kind, open, Midwestern face.

"Nice to meet you too, Airman Cohen. Both of you," she replied.

The major opened the folder and tugged reading glasses from an inside jacket pocket. He read for a few seconds then spoke, he eyes still directed toward the folder. "As you may know, the US Air Force moved your father here in April of 1998 as part of his consulting package, first implemented in October 1997 after thirty years' active service." He looked up at her as he removed his glasses and cleared his throat.

"And this means...?" Lily shifted uncomfortably.

"Well, it means that, in the event of your father's death, the property should revert back to the military. Actually, I've been sent to take your father's place as a consultant for the air force."

Silence fell as Lily absorbed what he was saying. As the truth set in, all Lily could think about was the IDBs. About how Flynn would react to dealing with this asshole.

She shook her head, trying to clear it. Wasn't this what she wanted? She did not want to step into her father's shoes. She was not a trained soldier. She was not even a trained pencil pusher for the government. She was a waitress, for goodness sake. Let this guy go to DC and see the president. Lily took a deep breath of relief. She didn't have to go. Her happy gaze fell on the major and she could see him watching, evaluating her. His head was cocked to one side, his mouth grim. What suddenly sent alarm coursing through her was the brilliant gleam of avarice in his eyes as he studied her. She looked to the aide and saw how anxious he was, even under the enforced stoicism of his military training and demeanor.

"*Should* revert back? What does that mean, exactly?"

The major coughed and lowered his gaze. "Well, it means that, although the air force set up the purchase and arranged the move, the mortgage was paid by your father. It is a tacit understanding that the property would be donated back to the military."

"A tacit understanding?" She frowned. "If my father paid for it, doesn't it belong to our family?"

Nilsson squirmed as though irritated. "Look here, Miss Dawson. This property has a certain strategic advantage that is very important to the air force. This is why we moved General Dawson here in the first place. Now, it just makes tactical sense that another air force liaison live and work here."

Lily screwed up her mouth thoughtfully. "And that would be you?"

He nodded. "Yes, ma'am. I'm honored to petition for the position. I'm sure my wife, Cleo, will enjoy New Mexico."

"Do you have children?" Lily relaxed back onto the chair, her mind whirling.

"No, we don't," he snapped, his fine control breaking down.

Lily's knee-jerk reaction was to fight this guy tooth and nail. First off, he was an ass. That was evident even this early in their acquaintance. Secondly, she felt for military wives and keenly remembered the isolation her mother had dealt with here, even when caring for Lily full time. Thirdly, the IDBs would probably start attacking Earth themselves if they had to deal with him.

Then she thought of Florida and her mother and their life there. And how, until the previous night, she had wanted so desperately to return to that life. She frowned and felt close to tears again. Now, it seemed as though that life might not exist any longer. Suddenly, alarmingly, everything had changed. Lily felt very much alone. She stiffened her spine, her sense of responsibility taking over. First things first, she had to deal with the Polar Purge. If Flynn could truly be believed, then a lot— the survival of humanity—was riding on what Lily did in the next twenty-four hours.

She brought her gaze up to look at the major, the skin all across her body puckering in fear. The survival of humanity. She stood abruptly, startling the two men, who scrambled gracelessly to their feet.

"Yes, Major, I understand what you are saying. As you can imagine, we are trying to get my father's affairs in order and disperse his personal effects among the family and staff. If you could give me two weeks to get everything finished, I believe we can revisit this issue." She set her mouth in a firm line as she awaited his response.

"But...Miss Dawson...we are ready to take possession immediately. I'm sure that the air force personnel can take care of packing up General Dawson's possessions and shipping them to you in..." He broke off as he tried to remember pertinent facts from the file. "Florida. We can ship them to Florida."

Lily made her face as impassive as possible. "Major Nilsson, while I appreciate the offer, I'd rather see to this myself as it allows me to feel close to my father. Closure, of a sort. I'm sure you can understand that."

Nilsson looked like a cornered rat, and Lily realized that he seemed to already know something about the Purge and that the IDBs were the answer. Hence the pressure. She almost confided in him but simply couldn't. She didn't trust him and certainly not with an issue this important. It didn't matter that they were on the same side... There was something that didn't sit right.

Nilsson sighed, as if in resignation. "How long do you need, Miss Dawson?"

"If you can give me two weeks, I think everything can be taken care of."

Nilsson looked at his aide and a message passed between them. The aide pulled a cell phone from his pocket and moved into the front hall.

"As you wish, Miss Dawson. Please be aware that I will be nearby, staying at Kirtland. I think it's less than sixty miles from here, so not too far." He reached into an inner jacket pocket and retrieved a card which he passed to Lily. "Here's my contact information. You can call at any time. Leave a message and I'll get back to you right away."

He placed his cap on his head with practiced ease, donned his sunglasses, and moved into the hallway, Lily following. She reached around him to open the screen door. He hesitated a moment, looking down the hall curiously, but he stepped through and moved to the steps. Airman Cohen was waiting by the car, still talking into his cell. He spied them on the porch, quickly signed off, and approached them.

Nilsson turned, one foot on the second step, and regarded Lily thoughtfully. "Please be aware, Miss Dawson, you may encounter some files, some folders marked confidential. We respectfully ask that you set them aside for us. They fall under the purview of national security and must be returned to the air force. I'm sure you are not aware of the specifics of your father's consultation duties, but please understand, they were of the utmost importance and red-level security. Do you understand me, Miss Dawson?"

Lily kept her face stoic as she answered. "Yes, sir. I understand completely. I will keep his files secure for the air force." But not necessarily for you, she thought spitefully.

Nilsson watched her another half minute or so but then turned and descended the steps and entered the waiting car. It drove off, slowly lumbering from the drive and out toward the main road, passing a truck that was turning onto the first part of the ranch road. Lily saw the truck's approach and felt like tearing out her short blond hair. The ranch was like Grand Central Station this morning, and she needed to get to the airport!

The tan Toyota truck crawled to a slow stop right in front of the house. Lily waited patiently as the driver sat in shadow a moment before stepping through the door, heavy black bag in hand. Her face lit as she recognized him.

CHAPTER THIRTEEN

"Oh, my God, Hawkeye? Is that you?" She raced down the steps and flung her arms about the tall, slender man. He stiffened and recoiled immediately from the embrace. One hand came up to smooth his dark, cropped hair.

"Oh, God, Hawk, I'm so sorry. I forgot. It's been so long since I've seen you! How are you?"

She paused breathlessly and waited. She knew Hawkeye, who was born with a communication disorder, at Asperger's level on the autism spectrum, would take a while to be able to speak to her, especially after that greeting. He did well.

"Hello, Lily," he said formally. "It's good to see you."

"And me, you. It's been almost five years, hasn't it?"

"Yes," he replied, screwing up his brow thoughtfully. "More. Five years and four months."

She smiled. Yes, he would know that. "And your mother? She's well?"

"My mother had gout two months ago. Women don't usually get gout, you know," he added.

Lily motioned for him to follow her into the house and as she turned, she spied a strange, but somehow familiar farmhand standing next to the paddock entrance. She squinted to see him better. "Hey, Hawkeye, can you wait here a minute?"

"Yes, I can wait," he answered, staring at the boards that made up the side wall of the house. He seemed to be organizing them visually.

Lily studied the farmhand as she approached, wondering why he was out here alone. He was dressed in the usual ranch hand garb, a long-sleeved cotton shirt and thick denim jeans atop leather work boots. He had long gray hair, tied back in a low ponytail and keen blue eyes shone from a weathered but plump face. Why was he familiar to her?

"I'm sorry," she said as she approached. "Do...do I know you?" She bit her lip, mind racing as she tried to place him.

He held out one hand and twisted it gently in the air. "You did the right...thing, Lily. We don't wish to...work...with the major. He is not of the...mindset...we need."

Shock jetted through Lily, making her knees weak. "Flynn?"

"Yes. You call me Flynn," he said softly. "Please, Lily, you must hurry. The leader will give you a token, a type of... contract, that you will bring back to us. We understand you have...contacted Collins."

"Yes, and I am going now to catch a plane to meet with the president. The leader."

"Good." He nodded and tilted his grizzled head as if listening. His attention shifted back to Lily. "Remember, liaison, we are always with you."

He turned and walked toward the barn. A blast of heat washed across Lily and he was gone.

She took a deep breath as her mind shut down a bit. This... these events were becoming more than she could handle. Wearily, she turned and walked back toward Hawkeye. Nervous, he had started his usual OCD activity, shaking the fingers of one hand together as he stepped from one foot to the other.

"I'm here, Hawk," she said, mounting the porch steps and approaching slowly. "Let's go inside and you can tell me why you're here."

Lily held the door open for him as they passed into the coolness of the house.

"Brookhouse Realty. I work for Brookhouse Realty," Hawkeye said loudly as Lanny approached them along the hallway.

"Hello, Hawkeye," Lanny said. He knew Hawk well, as they were of the same tribe, so he didn't offer to shake hands or approach too closely. "What brings you to Good Neighbor?"

Hawkeye looked at the floor as if counting the wooden boards as he responded. "I work for Brookhouse Realty and I take photographs for listings," he explained.

Lanny turned solemn eyes to Lily. "Is that so?" he said musingly. "Lily, truck's ready when you are—on the side," he said as he grabbed her bags that were resting beside the door.

"See you, Hawk," he said as he passed through the screen door.

Lily sighed and shook her head from side to side. "Come on, Hawk. Sage is going to have to show you around. I have a plane to catch, but I would love to visit with you when I get back in a few days, okay?"

Hawkeye smiled and looked shyly at Lily. "Okay!" he said with some enthusiasm. His face fell. "Do you hear that?"

Lily cocked her head to one and studied Hawkeye. "Hear what?"

"Vibration. It hurts my stomach," he replied, his gaze casting about the hallway. "I see a flash. A bright silver flash." His face was screwed into a huge grimace and he was stepping from foot to foot, hands flailing, clearly agitated. Lily was worried about his square black bag which was slipping down one arm.

"Whoa, Hawk," she said gently, reaching to gingerly touch his arm. She slid the heavy bag back onto his shoulder and started walking toward the kitchen, pulling him along with a gentle osmosis effect. He calmed as they entered the dimness of the kitchen, his attention caught by the new environment.

"Well, look who's here!" Sage exclaimed. "Hawkeye Tiva. How are you?"

Hawkeye's face lit in a self-conscious smile. He was clearly thrilled to see Sage. "Hello," he said, dipping his head shyly.

"Hawk is here to photograph the ranch for the realty listing," Lily said hurriedly.

Sage, compressing her lips in subtle disapproval, still picked up on Lily's need immediately. She turned a smile to Hawkeye and moved closer to him, clearly and adroitly changing his interest away from Lily.

"I'll be back as soon as possible," Lily whispered as she left the kitchen through the back door. She didn't say good-bye to Hawkeye, trying to avoid exciting him further.

"I saw your mother at the clinic last week," Sage was saying as Lily stepped out of earshot.

Outside the sun offered a full but slanting morning light. Lily relished the warm rays on her face as she rounded the house. Lanny was waiting for her, reading glasses perched on his nose and head tilted back as he perused the morning paper. He sensed her approach and peered at her over the glasses as she neared the truck. He folded the paper and set it aside as he folded and pocketed his glasses. "Is Hawkeye okay?" he asked as she closed the truck door.

"He's with Sage," she responded, eyeing the backseat to make sure her bag and suitcase were there.

Lanny nodded and handed her an egg and bacon biscuit wrapped in waxed paper. He leaned forward and switched on the ignition. Lily looked back once as they moved down the drive, her heart longing to stay at Good Neighbor. She realized suddenly that this was home. Her real home. The thought was disturbing and comforting at the same time.

CHAPTER FOURTEEN

"Which terminal?" Lanny asked as they approached the airport, which was just off I-25. Lanny switched on the turn signal and exited the highway.

"Umm, I dunno," Lily said. She reached into her front pocket and pulled out her phone. She quickly texted Collins. *At airport. Flight?*

The answer was almost immediate. *It'll be Southwest. Waiting to divert a plane. Sit tight.*

"He says Southwest," she told Lanny.

Lanny nodded and turned onto the access road that would take them by all the terminal check-ins. He pulled up at the Southwest awning and stopped. Lily scrambled out and reached for the back-cab door.

"I'll go park and come back to wait with you," Lanny said.

Lily hefted out her small suitcase and slung her large tote bag over one shoulder. She studied the dear face and spoke slowly, from a gut-level instinct. "Lanny, listen. You shouldn't stay here. You need to go back home and keep everything sane there. There's an air force guy that may come snooping around. Don't tell him anything. Play dumb, okay? Also…" Her voice faltered. "Stay away from all water. Boil it. Better yet, drink bottled soda. Stay on the ranch, away from people, if you can. Postpone what you can until I get back."

Lanny watched her, a frown marring his broad, heavy features. "But…water? I hear. I will. Will you call us while you're away? My Miss will make me crazy."

Lily smiled, close to tears. How she loved this man who accepted everything so calmly and seldom questioned.

"Yes. I will, every chance I get. I wish you guys would get cell phones. Sure would make my life easier."

Lanny grimaced. "You are lucky we have answering machines," he said.

Lily smiled and sniffed back tears. "I guess so. I'll…I'll be back as quick as I can."

"Be safe," he said and then added a long blessing in guttural Acoma Keres.

Lily closed the door, feeling somehow consecrated and comforted.

As she was entering the Southwest terminal, a small Native woman approached her. She was wearing a tailored gray broadcloth pantsuit over a crisp white blouse, her dark hair pulled neatly back into a bun. Military, Lily thought immediately. Beautiful, was her second, more pensive thought.

"Miss Dawson? My name is Hunter Moon. I was asked to contact you by Colonel Collins."

Lily smiled and the woman visibly relaxed, returning the smile. "It's very nice to meet you," Lily said.

"If you'll come this way, we have an area set aside for you to wait for your flight." She indicated a narrow passageway off to the left.

Lily followed her, marveling at how nondescript the disguised passageway was. No one, if not told, would ever think it led anywhere other than to janitorial and mechanical areas. Instead, at the end of a long hallway, they passed through opaque glass doors and into a well-appointed waiting room.

Two uniformed men raised their heads at her entry but quickly dropped their gazes. Hunter took the case from Lily's hand and led her to a computer station. She placed the case on the floor and rapidly tapped keys, then, with a reassuring smile, handed a headset to Lily. Lily put it on and sat in the chair as the screen flickered.

"Uncally!" Lily said happily as Colonel Collins's face appeared on the screen. He smiled, but his sedate green eyes regarded her worriedly.

"Hello, Peanut. You look none the worse for wear. Are you doing okay?"

"I am," she hastened to reassure him. "Things are a bit crazy, of course, but I'm putting one foot in front of the other, just the way you taught me to."

"That's my girl," he responded somewhat absently. "Listen, the plane should be touching down any minute. It'll be government issue, and you'll board through that side terminal like any usual flight, but then you'll be on the tarmac instead of the umbilical. It's the way it works. You ask Airman Moon for anything you need to make you more comfortable. Try to eat and rest, okay? When you get to the strip here in DC, a car will be there to pick you up and bring you here. Airman Moon will show you where to go and she'll take care of you. You can trust her."

"Where are you?" Lily asked. "Your office at the Pentagon?"

He lowered his gaze and his face grew pink. "Nah, they moved us to an underground bunker this morning. That's where you'll be coming. I'll meet you here."

Lily tried on a reassuring smile when his gaze lifted back to her. "Good. You'll be safe there."

He chuffed and shook his head. "I guess. Sure looks that way."

"Is Astrid with you?" Lily asked, suddenly concerned for his girlfriend's welfare. "Is she okay?"

He shook his head in the negative. "No, she's sick. She was working in Tennessee as the Purge headed this way. She has it so is in Bethesda hospital being treated." He must have seen her look of dismay. "She'll be okay. She has to," he said quickly. "She's getting the onslaught of the newest antivirals plus transfusions and she's on life support. By the way, you'll get some shots when you get here and they may examine you before they let you in. Just go with it."

Lily sighed. "This too shall pass," she said, using her father's favorite phrase.

Collins smiled warmly at her, his eyes growing sad. "I know you have to miss him. Especially now. I do too."

Lily shrugged. "Yeah. You know me, though...I fought it as long as I could."

He laughed hollowly and glanced down when a tone sounded. "Okay, Little Lil. They're ready for you. I'll see you in a few hours."

CHAPTER FIFTEEN

Traveling behind Hunter through a tall, paned-glass corridor was surreal. To her right was the regular terminal and she could see that a large portion of the travelers were ill or on the verge of becoming so. Their eyes were glued to the newsfeed screens whenever possible. She saw two people, a man and a young woman, vomiting into airport trash bins. Many people were coughing and walking around as though in a trance, some bleeding from their eyes or mouth. Lily had never felt as grateful as she did in that moment. There was some guilt involved, too. Because her father had been military and she'd been secluded back at the ranch because of his death…well, it was all a stroke of luck, really, that she was now being coddled and protected.

But she *was* trying to help save most of the people on the planet or at least in the US. Who knew why, exactly, that she had been chosen for this onerous task. But she had and she felt a real sense of duty. No matter what happened, she would let the higher power or powers guide her in the path she should take.

She sighed before stepping onto the accordion-like steps and into the plane.

"Hello, Miss," said an upbeat steward as he escorted her aboard and into the first of the ten or so plush seats. Empty seats. Were they going to fly alone? He reached across, murmuring apologies, and buckled her in.

"Thank you, Emmons," Hunter said as she entered the main cabin. She had stepped into the cockpit briefly, presumably checking in with the pilots. "We'll have lunch once we're at altitude."

She sat in the seat across the aisle from Lily and buckled in.

"Yes, ma'am," the steward responded before shutting the cabin door and securely fastening it. He buckled himself into one of the front, rear-facing seats and smiled at Lily before picking up a magazine. Almost immediately the plane started moving. Lily didn't have time to indulge in her usual angst about flying before they were smoothly airborne.

Hunter sighed audibly when they reached altitude. "Well, we're on the way," she said with some relief as her brown eyes studied Lily. "I'm not a huge fan of flying."

"And you in the air force!" Lily laughed. "I'm not fond of it either, but I have to say, flying this way is better."

Hunter nodded and her smile faltered. "Yes, especially right now," she replied softly.

Lily leaned forward. "Is your family safe?"

Tears abruptly sprouted in the airman's eyes and she rapidly blinked them away. "We're Acoma and they're mostly up at a village on top of a mesa. I so hope they'll be safe there."

"I know the village," Lily said reassuringly. "My...family... is that pueblo too. They are pretty isolated. Maybe it will pass them by."

Hunter's eyes grew wide and she glanced at Lily's short blond hair. "You're not Acoma."

"No, not by birth. But I was pretty much raised by a Native couple. Landon and Sage Kya'nah."

"Ah, I know Sage. She and my mother birthed together at Falcon Lodge and they've been like sisters. You must be from the family she worked for. How do I not know you?"

"Oh, I've been away for a while," Lily explained. "Which one of her children were you born with?"

"Just after Sibby," Hunter replied, her eyes shining.

"Uh-oh," Lily said with a chuckle. The Kya'nahs' middle child, a daughter named Cibola, was a famous prankster. Lily had only hung out with her about a half dozen times since Sibby attended pueblo school, but those times had been fraught with mischief. "What is she doing now? Still at the university?"

Hunter shook her head. "Oh no, she left there about three-four years ago. She's married now, fat and happy with two babies. Her husband, Blain, works at the casino."

"Blain? She hated him in school!" Lily said.

Hunter laughed and shrugged.

"Here you go, ladies," Emmons said as approached with a covered tray. He braced his feet against the seat posts and laid the cover on an empty seat. He pointed with an index finger and Lily realized there was a tray table fitted into the wall next to her. Hunter already had hers down so Emmons served her first.

The meal was an excellent presentation—chicken cordon bleu with sides of asparagus and new potatoes. It was even served with a roll as well as real cutlery and cloth napkins. Lily, not all that hungry yet, stared at the meal in amazement as Emmons placed a glass bottle of soda on her little table.

"Is this the president's plane?" she asked.

Hunter laughed and covered her full mouth with one hand. "Sort of. It's for visiting dignitaries."

Lily lifted one eyebrow in response and then started eating, her appetite growing with each delicious bite. She realized after some time that the airman was watching her.

"Your mission must be important," Hunter said finally. She didn't seem to be fishing for information. The question was presented in a purely conversational tone.

Lily placed her fork perpendicular to her plate. What could she tell her? Collins had said she could trust her. Yet a deep-seated knowledge that the fewer who knew of Flynn the better held her tongue.

"It's about the Purge. I have information that could prove important," she replied carefully.

Hunter nodded reflectively. "I figured it was something like that."

A shiny, black, very familiar type of car awaited Lily and Hunter on the secluded tarmac at a private hangar in DC. Standing atop the stairway, Lily turned to Hunter and sighed. "No airport?"

Hunter shook her head. "Not here. Too populated."

Lily held herself straighter and smoothed the hem of her shirt. "Here we go," she said.

The two women disembarked, walked across a broad expanse of concrete, and settled into the backseat as the driver shut the door and took his seat.

It had been a long time since Lily had been to this city and she enjoyed the sights as the car crawled through traffic. A short time later, as she spied the Smithsonian Museum buildings, the windows gradually darkened until she could no longer see through them.

"We're going to a secure location," Hunter explained. "Don't worry. It's okay."

A smoky barrier lifted from the back of the two seats in front of them and a prerecorded voice informed them that for their own protection, a blackout mode had been implemented.

Nervousness rose in Lily and she clenched her hands together to keep them from trembling.

Although she and Hunter had chatted in a very relaxed mode during the flight, they were now entering the inner sanctum of the United, for God's sake, States of America. And people were falling sick in droves.

The car paused for a long beat then took a nauseating lurch and Lily sensed that they were going in a circular motion. A wave of carsickness washed across her and she leaned her head back and closed her eyes.

She wondered what would be expected of her and she longed for Flynn so she could be reassured and also get more questions answered. All this was happening so quickly. How could one Florida trailer park rat help conquer a possible worldwide pandemic?

The circular motion stopped abruptly, as did the car, and Lily cautiously opened one eye. Everything was still dark, but the car started moving forward again, very slowly. Hunter reached across the seat and held Lily's hand reassuringly.

They traveled this way for many minutes. Being in the dark this way was screwing with Lily's time sense so she wasn't sure how long. Hunter was humming under her breath and Lily recognized it as a light tune Sage often hummed as she worked around the house. It was comforting for her to hear it now, under these frightening conditions.

CHAPTER SIXTEEN

The car finally rolled to a stop and the engine switched off. Lily sat upright, still fighting nausea, as the door opened. Dim light flooded the backseat and the driver announced cheerfully, "Here we are, safe and sound." Lily had a sudden, irrational urge to stomp his foot as she left the vehicle but managed to behave herself.

She and Hunter stepped into a huge cavern-like structure, man-made of concrete and steel, filled with an assortment of military vehicles, from dirty, mud-spattered jeeps to sleek, black sedans. There were even two stretch limos visible from where they stood. The driver escorted them toward a small, but thick-looking steel door. He swiped a card and waited. The trio stood awkwardly until the door opened and only Lily and Hunter were ushered in by a short, blond army private and led to an elevator opposite the outer door.

During the ride, Lily studied the private, noting how his eyelashes and brows were a pale yellow color, perfectly matched to his light blond hair. Hunter followed suit, then, catching her eye, indicated that she too had noted the man's coloring, a very unusual sighting in their New Mexico home. Lily smiled, some of her tension easing. She was awfully glad she wasn't totally alone on this journey.

They stopped at a floor labeled Processing and the private led them through a series of small enclosed cubicles, each bathed with a different colored light. Next, they stepped into a clinic-like area and two medical personnel—she was never sure whether they were physicians or nurse practitioners or even nurses—took their vital signs and administered three shots to each of them. Then, after her tote bag was searched and sanitized, their temperatures were taken a second time, blood was drawn from one arm, and they stepped through a wind tunnel and then into another elevator.

The elevator stopped quickly and opened into a tornado of efficiency. Human bodies moved and interlaced in a torrent of movement. Dark blue uniforms and a myriad of combat garb were in the majority, but they were interspersed with some civilian wear. The huge concourse they stepped into was mostly silent, filled with only the sound of shuffling or tapping feet and the occasional murmured statement. People moved seamlessly around Lily and Hunter as though they were mere rocks dividing a busy stream.

And then Colonel Collins was approaching, in his blue combat wear, followed by a cadre of blue suits. As soon as he was close enough, he lifted Lily into his arms and peered closely at her face, her feet dangling above the polished floor.

"Oh, *man*, it is good to see you," he exclaimed before finally settling her back onto her feet. He shook hands with the airman and thanked her for escorting Lily to DC. He turned back to Lily, who, seeing him surrounded by a small sea of indulgent smiles but worried eyes, felt a deep sense of surrealism nibble at her.

"So, POTUS will see you in," he glanced at his watch, "I think it's just a bit less than half an hour now."

Lily frowned. "POTUS?"

He laughed shortly and began herding her along the hallway. "What rock have you been under? It's a nickname for the pres. Means President of the United States."

"Ahh," Lily muttered.

"Sir?"

Collins turned back to Hunter. "Yes, Moon?"

"I've been mustered back to Air Six."

He nodded. "I'm sure. Would you like a moment?"

"Yes, sir," she answered.

Collins shoved Lily toward Hunter, who took both her hands in a firm grip. "I need to go, Lily. It's been a pleasure."

Lily's mouth opened to protest—how could she be alone in this environment—but Hunter interjected.

"It's not because I want to leave you alone. I need to pick up some other people who need to be protected. You understand?"

Lily did and her gaze rose to meet Hunter's warm brown eyes. "I do," she responded. "Thank you for everything, and please, be safe out there."

Hunter smiled widely and surreptitiously pulled the corner of a white facemask from her jacket pocket. "From the clinic. I have gloves too," she whispered, glancing to Collins, who was conferring with an aide. "You know, just in case."

"Remember, it's the water," Lily whispered.

"I know. I only drink packaged stuff from a few months ago," she replied. "I know fresh water is usually better for us…"

Lily shrugged in response. "Not these days."

"I may see you on the way home. I hope I do," she added. "You protect yourself, regardless. Especially watch the water—everywhere. The people in the clinic can outfit you too. Go ahead and let them. If you vomit…get diarrhea or get dizzy, even a little, you go to the hospital right away, okay? They'll transfuse you before the damage sets in. Promise me."

Lily squeezed the hand she still held. "I will. I promise." She pulled Hunter into a brief embrace, then gasped as Hunter pressed soft lips to her cheek. Stirred by the innocent kiss, she watched Hunter walk away along the corridor.

Collins was suddenly next to her. "Come with me, Lily. We don't want to keep the president waiting."

"No, sir," Lily said with a sigh. "What's he like? POTUS, I mean."

"You'll like him. We went to school together, graduate school. He's a good guy."

The entire entourage, with Collins and Lily in front, moved along a bare but well-lit hallway. After walking for more than half a mile, they paused at a heavy wooden double doorway. One of the aides punched a code into a keypad set into the wall and the door opened. The next hallway was warmer, Lily noticed, as well as more finished structurally. As they progressed through several more doorways, Lily wondered about the extent of this secure facility. They had surely traveled miles in a linear direction and had passed many long hallways stretching out along either side.

Collins was unusually quiet, occasionally murmuring answers to whispered questions posed by their electronics-obsessed following. Lily's nervousness, in his presence, began to abate somewhat. It was as though his calm demeanor had passed on to her. He reminded her of her father in so many ways.

The group passed into a cavernous room, a dome, with curved steel struts that met in the middle above their heads. Several sofas and chair conversation areas dotted the room and cases of bottled water and rations were stacked along the perimeter.

Lily's eyes were drawn to the left where a large wooden desk rested on a Persian rug, surrounded by chairs and a tribe of suits. A man sat there in shirtsleeves, tie askew, and it took her only seconds to recognize President David Anderson. He glanced up from the paper he was perusing, which, of course, drew all eyes their way.

Collins led them across the room toward the desk, removing his billed hat and tucking it under one arm. He shook the president's offered hand.

"Mr. President, this is Lily Dawson."

"Ahh, Ducky's girl. It's very nice to meet you. How was your trip out? Did you have everything you needed?" He studied her with clear hazel eyes, more topaz than green.

Though intimidated by his palpable charisma, she took the proffered hand and shook it. "It was good. Thank you."

"You're very welcome." He looked at the worried-looking men surrounding him. "Gentlemen, let's take a break."

With a collective sigh and murmurs of curiosity, the advisors dispersed into small groups, a short distance from the desk area. Lily turned and noticed that Uncally's group had backed away as well.

CHAPTER SEVENTEEN

President Anderson indicated two of the chairs next to his desk and waited as Lily and Collins seated themselves.

"Well," Anderson said as he resumed his seat and leaned back in his chair. "You've been vetted by the crew, I'm sure, but I have to ask you—you were contacted by the IDB E-One?"

Lily blinked slowly. "No, sir. I was contacted by an IDB that my father called Flynn." She shifted nervously. Had she made a mistake coming here? Was this all some kind of joke? A dream? She wished for wakefulness.

The president nodded. "I see. And this Flynn. Can you describe him?"

Lily felt her cheeks pinken. For some odd reason, she had not expected this third-degree questioning. But she should have, she supposed. She clasped her hands together to keep them from trembling. "Well, that's hard to say. She changes…appearance. I…I think she's come to me as…a little boy, a woman, and an old man. I know that sounds weird…"

Collins reached out and rubbed his large palm along her back. It was a reassuring gesture.

The president nodded again and a smile stretched across his face. "It's okay, Lily. I believe you." He leaned forward and clasped his hands together on his desk. "Now, tell me what this Flynn wants of you. Of us."

Collins cleared his throat. "Should I leave, Mr. President? I think this is above my clearance."

The president considered Collins, his gaze steady. "Colonel Collins, Alan. You understand that in times of national crisis, certain shortcuts are taken. We studied your file when you first contacted us, and I can find no evidence that you would want to harm your country in any way. Therefore, we have raised your classification and the paperwork has been sent. But I will say this…"

Lily took in a deep breath as she watched the president's affable mien change into a feral face with steely, no-nonsense eyes.

"Nothing. And I repeat, nothing shared here today will leave this room. Do you understand, Colonel? Miss Dawson?"

"I do, sir. And in my capacity as Lily's unofficial guardian since her father's death, I give you my solemn promise that she can always confide in me with the utmost confidence and security."

The president looked at Lily, his gaze warming. "Yes, Colonel, and I think she will appreciate your help during this trying time. She will need your support."

"Yes, Mr. President," Collins responded quietly.

"Now, Lily. Please tell me exactly what the IDB told you."

Lily straightened her shoulders and began to speak in a low voice, telling the president and Collins everything from her first encounter with Flynn all the way up to boarding the plane for the flight to Washington.

Both men pondered her words in silence when she finished.

"Oh, my God," Collins muttered finally.

"Yes," President Anderson agreed. He rose and paced in short bursts of distance behind his desk. "I've read all the data but hearing it this way… I wondered if they were real. I mean, the others, well, of course, but the…" He paused, and recoiled as though saying too much.

"Mr. President, I think it's gone airborne. It's had to, to spread this fast. And even with water, it's gonna spread like cholera does," Collins said quietly. "What if it gets beyond this continent? Goes worldwide?"

The president fingered his chin thoughtfully. "No, just water, not air. Not yet. The first reports indicate it is viral, as Lily has said, so it's even more virulent and harder to contain. It causes what's called a clotting storm in the body. It affects everyone, especially the young and the old. Yes, this has to stop here. If our allies find out...well."

He sat abruptly and pulled open a desk drawer. He scribbled a few words, then motioned one of the four-star generals over and handed him a note. "Now, we wait," he said. "You know, nothing like this has happened since I took office. I'm just glad we have protocol in place."

Lily nodded that she'd heard him, then wrung her hands and glanced around. She noted that Collins's people, who had gathered to one side, out of hearing distance, had turned as one unit when the general approached the desk. The remaining members of the president's entourage had leapt to alertness as well, and several of them, obviously Secret Service, were talking rapidly into wristbands. The air was suddenly charged and this only increased Lily's edginess.

Collins patted her hand as a side door slid slowly open and an elderly man stepped into the cavernous room. He saluted the president and approached slowly, limping heavily on one leg. "Mr. President?" he said, in a low, raspy voice.

The president had risen and returned the salute. Now he offered his hand to the newcomer, who was, Lily saw, a very rare five-star general. He had served his country well. She was held spellbound by the heavy medals on his chest and the circular insignia on the epaulets of his dark blue air force uniform.

"General Ford. Good to see you, sir," President Anderson said in greeting. "We have a situation of some urgency and will need a chip, sir."

General Ford glanced at Lily and Collins, then back to the president. "Yes, sir. You do understand that there are only two left," he said in a low, almost inaudible tone.

The president looked momentarily concerned, but he visibly strengthened his stance and pulled on a very good poker face. "I was not aware of that, General Ford, but there are few, if any other options at this point."

"The CDC report says four hundred thousand and rising by the day," Ford agreed. "Is there a plan in place?"

President Anderson nodded. "Yes, a good one, I believe."

"Well, that's good enough for me," General Ford said, smiling wide enough to reveal perfect dentures. "Let's save America, sir."

He reached into his front breast pocket and removed a slim metal case. The case was so polished that it caught and shot the ceiling lights as he moved it. He pressed a recessed button and the lid opened slowly. Ford gingerly reached two fingers inside and his hand shook, whether from age or fear, Lily couldn't discern. He gasped slightly when his fingers encountered their target and Lily suddenly understood the tremor of repressed energy that vibrated his form. He withdrew an oversized coin, a flat, patterned disc, from the case. It was slightly larger than a half-dollar but was oddly domed—convex—on both sides.

The president extended one hand, his face curious. "Do you know, I've been in this office a little more than two years now and this is the first time we've had to resort to this."

Ford nodded in understanding. "Enemies abound, sir."

He laid the disc on the president's palm, and Lily lurched in alarm when the president's knees buckled. Ford and Collins both, uncharacteristically, caught hold of Anderson to support him and keep him from falling. Secret Service men descended on them, only to be waved back by their gasping leader.

"Steady on, sir," General Ford said, relinquishing his hold and stepping back. "I should have warned you about the effect."

"Quite all right, Ford. I understand." His face grew thoughtful as he sat heavily. "Thank you for this." He gestured with the hand that held the token. "You can resume now."

"Mr. President," General Ford murmured, with a departing salute.

CHAPTER EIGHTEEN

The president returned the salute and Ford retreated. He looked down and studied the token. Lily could now see that it covered his entire palm, and it glimmered with a strange luminosity. Much as Flynn had glowed in her bedroom.

Lily sighed. "Thank you, sir, for enabling this." She held out both hands and accepted the disk from him. Power coursed through her body, making it hum, and she was exceedingly glad she was sitting down.

"I had little choice, Lily." He captured her gaze with his and perused her carefully, as if making sure, one final time, that she was trustworthy. "How does Flynn contact you?"

Lily studied him and debated sharing what Flynn had told her about traveling in glass. She couldn't bring herself to tell him more. She had the feeling suddenly that what she and Flynn had was insular and not for sharing. It was a hunch and she followed it. "It's okay, sir. I promise that you have nothing to fear from me."

"So, what now, Lily. What happens next?"

Lily shrugged. "I go home, well, back to New Mexico. I will give this to Flynn and ask her to implement the cure. That's about it."

"How long will that take?" Collins asked in a low tone.

"I don't know, Uncally. I will ask her next time I see her and let you both know."

"Yes, we're going to give you a ScrambleText service so you can send us encrypted updates by cell phone. They'll go directly to my aide. His name is Wendell. You can trust him completely. His clearance is almost as high as mine." The president chuckled at his own joke before sobering. "Do you need water?"

Lily thought of the cool well water at the ranch and knew she couldn't trust it anymore.

As if reading her thoughts, Collins answered for her. "We're installing an antiviral lighting unit at the ranch, at the water intake. The light kills the virus upon contact, even through water. I think the crew is already there."

The president nodded thoughtfully. "Ten minutes at a full boil and a microfilter, Lily, if untreated by the light. That's what they are telling us. Pass the word along please."

"But without telling anyone about this meeting," Collins warned quietly.

Lily heard a noise and saw that a long line of new suits had gathered in the room. They were shifting impatiently, and all had a haggard, fearful air about them.

"Yes," she agreed quickly, getting to her feet as the president stood and extended his hand. "We'll be on our way, Mr. President, sir. I'm sure you have enough on your plate. I will do whatever I can."

"Thank you, Lily. To whom much is given, much is required," he responded, eyes suddenly empty and desolate against the clear skin of his face. "Please let Wendell know if you need anything. And take care of yourself. Godspeed."

"And you, sir. Stay safe."

He nodded and released her hand. Lily and Collins walked toward the entrance as the hordes of suits descended on the president.

"I'd so hate to be him," Lily muttered, glancing back at the swarm.

"You got that right," Collins agreed.

Lily fingered the disc in her jeans pocket and tried not to listen as Collins set up travel arrangements with the staff of three who'd followed them from the room. As a five-man unit, they navigated the same elevator and hallways they'd entered through until they came to the anteroom next to the parking area.

Collins sighed loudly and paused at the entrance. "Lily, I hate this. Are you sure that you want to take on this huge task of being the liaison? It's gotta be incredibly frightening for you."

Lily smiled and rested one hand on his forearm. "I already am taking it on, Uncally, and there's not much I can do about it. I am surprised though, that POTUS gave it up so easy. I really expected more resistance. I mean, he doesn't know me from Adam."

Collins sighed again. "You have to understand, Lily. Your father was very well respected. Everyone, the past president and even this new one, knows what sacrifices he'd made to be the liaison." He fell silent, his mien thoughtful. "I admit. I didn't realize to what extent."

Lily studied him, head cocked to one side. "How do you mean?"

Collins shook himself, as if shedding morose thoughts. "I realize now why he left DC so abruptly. Isolated himself. I guess I'd always wondered about it. Look, we'll talk later. You need to go. People are dying as we stand here."

Lily nodded, pressing her lips in a thin line. "Thank you. For everything." She hugged him briefly as an aide opened the door.

"I expect to hear from you every day. Every morning. I mean it." He leaned through the doorway after she'd passed through.

"I love you, Uncally," Lily said as she clambered into the backseat that awaited her.

"Love you too," he called out as the driver closed the car door. "Be safe."

Lily felt tears well as she settled back into the plush upholstery next to her luggage and hugged her bag to herself. She wished he could come home with her. She wished he could be the one to deal with Flynn and saving the world.

The disc vibrated against her thigh, heating the flesh even through the pocket. She pressed one hand against it, through her jeans, and it stilled in response.

CHAPTER NINETEEN

Journal entry
October 21, 2016
Flynn came to me during the night. It says that all is well but that they are watching a threat in the Middle East. There is a small gathering of anti-American expatriates from here. They hate America's sense of imperialism and one of them has some history in explosives…

Journal entry
September 11, 2017
Heard from Lily today finally. She's doing well. San is still drinking though and this is the burden I bear. Though Lily would never tell me about it, the service watching her and San reported that San went out drinking with Claire Wright and Steven Bibb. They all got drunk and Claire and Steven took off, stranding San at a bar. Luckily the bar owner knew San and called the RV park. Lily had to go pick her up.

Lily raised her eyes from the tablet. She and her mom were being watched? Creepy. Lily had never noticed anyone, but that didn't mean much. Though probably stereotypical in dress and mannerisms, private detectives were good at being invisible. She was surprised her father hadn't told her, however. When the family had stepped off the ranch, it had been common for one of the paid bodyguards to accompany them. But Lily had believed that all surveillance had stopped once she and her mother moved from there and essentially out of her father's daily life.

> *Journal entry*
> *February 14, 2018*
> *Doesn't seem like Valentine's Day without the girls here, though I sent Lily a card. I admit to some despondency because I so wish to be with them but I have to stay strong.*
> *I will soon need to retire from this position and install a new liaison. I dread it, the uncertainty of how someone might react to this reality. Flynn and I have talked about it but I fear approaching anyone. It would have to be someone who was willing to live near here, to isolate himself to a large degree and that's not easy to find.*
> *I must be a coward.*

She closed the journal and felt the low thrum of the token against her leg. She pressed her palm to it, as if comforting a small beast. It calmed somewhat.

Reading her father's journal was giving her great insight into his emotional life and how the IDB collective repeatedly had helped preserve life on Earth. The power of the energy cooperative was immense. So immense that it made clear how accidental, how weak humans were. She idly wondered about the structure of its existence. Flynn called it a collective, but Lily wondered if there was some type of hierarchical structure within. She sighed. There were so many questions.

Reaching up, Lily switched on the overhead light and examined the empty glass in front of her. The cabin steward, Johnny, had retreated to the front, and she was all alone in the body of the small airplane. Johnny had told her it was a relatively new Learjet 60 XR. He talked about it in hushed awe-filled whispers, amazing Lily. It *was* very nice, and Lily could easily see it being used to transport important people around the country, fuel costs be damned.

Her gaze roamed the dozen empty seats behind her and then came back to the glass. Did she dare? Hesitantly she reached and held the glass in both palms. Nothing happened. She closed her eyes and thought of Flynn.

Feeling foolish, she muttered a summons under her breath. "Flynn, come to me. Come to me, Flynn."

The glass shuddered between her palms, causing the remaining cubes of ice to clink together. She gasped, releasing it and leaning backward. For a brief moment, she saw Flynn in the surface of the glass and then, in an instant, the IDB was sitting across the aisle from her. Though in the glass it was a silver-haired female, it appeared there as a man, dressed in a black business suit. His hair was curly but cropped close, and his middle-aged brown eyes studied Lily questioningly.

"Did you get it?"

"Hello, Flynn. Yes, I did." She reached into her pocket and retrieved the token.

Flynn cocked his head to one side and studied it. "Time means little to...us," he reminded her. "But these tokens are older than your Earth. Our people began as such, millions of your centuries ago."

Lily frowned. "How do you mean? Began as such?"

He reached out and his hand drew the metal of the token disk into the very flesh of it. There was a sad, forlorn coldness on her palm where it had rested.

"We were not as you...your planet...in the beginning. We spun through space as...nomads... Like this." He indicated the hand that had absorbed the token. "It was who we were. Then the planet Niruu swept us into a...vortex and we collided with a primitive, barely-formed Earth. Our energy transformed it for many millions of your years, until Niruu returned once again on its orbit. There came a great energy wave during that passage and our people were...swept away. It was then we...splintered back into space but we…remain trapped within Earth's magnetic… fields. We continue to exist alongside you."

Lily's mouth had fallen open a bit. She closed it and moistened her tongue before speaking. "Always? I mean, can you leave Earth and travel through space?"

Flynn nodded. "Yes, now? Somewhat. We do not go as far as before. We are…nomads…no longer."

"And this is okay with you?"

Flynn shrugged. "The energy is everything. What you believe, you will become. It is better to travel well than to arrive, as one of your wise leaders said."

There was a subtle sound from the other side of the curtain. Lily leaned closer. "So, will you be able to save us with that token?" she whispered.

A flash of heat heralded Flynn's disappearance. But it wasn't entirely gone. It…she…was staring at Lily from the glass. "Yes," she answered, her voice made crystalline by the glass encasing her. "We will treat the water immediately."

Lily felt bereft after Flynn left the glass. She stood and made her way to the small lavatory at the back of the plane. Inside, she stared at herself in the mirror for a long, pondering moment.

The crazy things that had happened to her in the space of just one week bordered on the insane. She still couldn't wrap her mind around the reality of IDBs. That they existed and that they interacted in her own reality. And the Greys. Who were they really and why target Earth? Was it really only for the ore? Why wipe out Earthlings—why not enslave them as workers?

She had so many questions and very few answers. Looking at herself, she made a vow to be tougher. To be more connected.

CHAPTER TWENTY

Life back at Good Neighbor Ranch was much as before when she returned. The only visual difference was a low broad platform behind the house. Located just above the well, it was no doubt the water purifier Collins had mentioned.

"Quite an addition," Sage said. She moved close to Lily and peered through the kitchen window with her.

"It's to clean the water," Lily explained quietly.

"I know. The men who installed it had a letter from your godfather."

"Good." Lily turned from the window and saw that Sage had prepared a full breakfast for her. "I met Hunter Moon, by the way. She says hello."

Sage smiled. "A good girl. Good to her family."

"You're not eating?" Lily asked as she took her usual seat.

Sage had crossed to the sink and was gazing pensively out the window above it. "No, not hungry."

Lily shrugged and sliced into a poached egg.

"Did you get any sleep?" Sage asked after many minutes had passed.

"Yes. Better than I expected," she replied. Lanny had dropped her at the front door just after midnight and Lily had dropped into bed, grateful to be home but exhausted by the events of the day.

"Good," Sage said. She coughed loudly.

Lily turned in alarm and studied Sage. "Are you okay, Saysay?"

Sage turned tired eyes on her. "Sure. Sure, I am. Are you through?"

Lily handed her the mostly empty plate, her gaze searching Sage's face for any signs of illness. "Only drink the water here at the ranch, okay?"

Sage's gaze peered through Lily. "Okay," she said simply.

Later, a frustrated Lily slammed her phone into the pocket of her denim overshirt and angrily chewed on a fingernail. No one was answering at any of her home numbers and she was terrified. She fished a cigarette from her jeans pocket and lit up, leaning her head back into the porch rocker. How sick was her mother? Had she succumbed to the Purge? She sighed. Why was *no one* answering? It was a business, for Goddess' sake, an RV park. Someone should answer. And don't forget that the voice mail is full, she reminded herself.

Her phone chimed and she eagerly wrestled it from her pocket. It was a message from Collins and she didn't know whether to be relieved or angry that it wasn't Florida calling.

So, did you make it home okay? Collins asked.

Yes, sorry I didn't text. Was late.

That's OK.

Hey, I can't get hold of Mama. Do you know anything?

Was she sick?

Lily pulled her bottom lip between her teeth. *Yes, in the hospital.*

Okay. I will check on her. Anything else you need?

No. The water thingie has been installed, BTW.

Good. Still. Soda n juices still a good idea. Nothing after 6-20 though. Look for production dates, not use by dates, ok?

Lily sighed nervously. Damn this mess. *Okay. Hey, Sage is coughing.*

How bad?

I haven't heard her for a while.

We can come get her. Bring her to the hospital here.

Lily mulled this idea a minute. *I'll keep an eye out n let u know, ok?*

OK. Be safe. Was the package delivered?

Lily realized suddenly that knowing the answer to this question had to be his primary reason for texting. He had POTUS to report to. *Yes. It will be opened right away.*

Good. He signed off by texting her a heart and she was impressed with his emoticon skills. He never failed to amaze her.

After a few moments, she realized Sage had come out onto the porch. She had a dishcloth dangling from one hand, but her gaze was unfocused and she seemed to be thinking faraway thoughts.

"Sage?" Lily questioned. There was no response, but Sage's breathing seemed harsh and labored. "Oh, my God. Come here," Lily whispered, taking Sage gently by the arms and pushing her down into a chair. "Let me get Lanny and we'll get you to the airport."

Knowing timely movement was imperative, Lily raced around the side of the house and toward the paddock, screaming Lanny's name as loudly as possible. She saw him then, racing toward her from the feed barn. She stopped and waved both arms over her head making sure he could see her. After agonizing moments, he reached her, panting heavily, his features sheened with sweat.

"It's Sage. You gotta help her."

Lanny was racing toward the house even before Lily had finished talking, so she ran alongside him. Sage was where she'd left her, still looking around as if dazed.

"Sage! Sage!" Lanny cried out. He took her by the shoulders and shook her roughly. A wide stream of blood gushed from one side of her mouth, and Lily's heart stopped.

"Lanny," she squeaked out. "Uncally says he can fly her to the hospital there. They can treat this."

Sage seemed to awaken somewhat from the daze and her eyes traveled from Lily to her husband. One hand brought the dishtowel up and dabbed at the blood, smearing it across her chin. "No. Home," she said in a raspy, oddly deep voice.

"Please, Miss. Let them help you there," Lanny said, his voice whimpering in a way Lily had never heard from him before.

She shook her head vigorously and her eyes began to glaze again. "Die home," she reiterated.

Harsh sobs shook Lanny as he lifted Sage from the chair, cradling her gently in his arms.

"Wait for me," Lily cried as she ran into the house and grabbed her bag from the hall table where she'd left it the night before. She turned the lock on the door and slammed it closed then leapt off the porch to help Lanny lift Sage into the truck. Lily crawled in the passenger side and held Sage upright as Lanny climbed in and gunned the engine.

The trip across the desert lands was a blur as Lily used the towel to gently clean Sage's face, cooing to her to try to help the older woman maintain consciousness. Her breathing was deteriorating rapidly, however, and fear tore through Lily's gut, making her breathless as well. She couldn't lose Sage, too, she just couldn't. Lanny was taking a shortcut to bypass the interstate, racing across Laguna Pueblo land to pick up Route 23 which would take them south to Sky Village.

"I can't...I can't...we need the hospital," Lily murmured, tears coursing along her face. "She...the water, Lanny. The water makes us sick. She needs to have her blood changed." She glanced toward Lanny and found his face a grim, skeletal mask. He didn't speak and she turned her attention back to Sage.

Soon Lily spied Enchanted Rock and then the twin boulders, as large as skyscrapers, that demarcated the entrance to the Kya'nahs' home village. A bit farther and they arrived at the informal checkpoint that marked entry onto Acoma private land. Lanny killed the engine, as a gesture of respect, and they waited, Lily shifting in her seat impatiently. Sage had fallen into a deep sleep, but her labored breathing filled the truck's cabin. Lanny rested one hand on hers, as if connecting and comforting her even as she struggled.

After about ten minutes, a very long ten minutes, a truck approached along the road to the village. Lanny stepped from his truck and closed the door. Lily craned her neck forward and watched as Lanny spoke to the driver of the other truck. Seconds later a young Native man moved to Lanny's truck and opened Lily's door. He and Lanny gently shoved Lily out and away as they lifted Sage's limp form and carried it to the other truck. Lily followed helplessly until Lanny gripped her shoulder and stilled her.

"Take the truck home. You can do nothing else. She is in the hands of our healers now."

His jet eyes watched her compassionately, his face still grim and stoic.

"Y...yes," Lily gasped. "I love her, Lanny. I do," she muttered sorrowfully.

He pulled her into a brief hug, and then he was gone, a trail of smoky dust following the truck up the trail. She watched it until it settled then walked back to Lanny's truck. She realized her face was dripping with the sobless tears she'd unknowingly shed. The tears came from the deepest recesses of her being. She realized suddenly as she sat in Lanny's truck, gripping the steering wheel in both hands, that she very well may have lost everything that was important to her. She turned the key in the engine, her heart heavy and thumping sluggishly in her chest as grief overwhelmed her.

CHAPTER TWENTY-ONE

A sob finally tore from Lily's throat as she awakened from a deep, dark place. A scent inundated her, a strange metallic smell, like heated steel. She couldn't remember anything—her mind was a black void—yet somehow she felt weighed down by extreme sadness. She swallowed cautiously and cracked open her eyelids. The light was dim. That seemed odd to her. She had a thought...a memory...of brightness. Opening her eyes fully, she stared up at an unfamiliar ceiling. A silvery metal ceiling that swirled with strange pale patterns.

Alarm raced through her and she raised up, pivoting herself. Her calves skirted a ledge and she realized that she was in a metal tank, sitting on a metallic platform. Dizziness washed across her and she gagged briefly. Composing herself, steeling herself, she stood, bracing herself against the nearest metal wall. Confused, she tried to take stock of her situation. Memory was returning slowly, but she had no idea how she'd come to be in this place.

A door was located off center on the far wall. She pushed off the wall she'd been leaning against and staggered toward it. It was only about a ten-foot journey, but she was exhausted and breathing heavily by the time she reached the door. There was no recognizable knob, so she pounded the door weakly with her fists, then tried to pry the oddly configured hinge. When it took too much effort to figure out how it moved, she rolled away, bracing her shoulders against the wall next to the door. She studied her prison, a solid metal box with nothing inside it except the ledge, a type of hard sleeping surface.

"Focus, Dawson," she muttered to herself. Sweeping both hands across her face, she tried to get her bearings and understand her surroundings. Light was filtering in from somewhere. She traced the light to tiny vertical slits located at intervals around the top of the box. Probably intended for ventilation as well as light. Was the box inside a bigger structure? Or outside? The air was still with no breeze, so there was no way to be sure.

She made her way shakily back to the ledge and sat. Her stomach rumbled and she wondered suddenly how long she'd been imprisoned. She realized that in addition to being hungry, she was also thirsty and very, very warm. She glanced down, relieved to see familiar T-shirt and jeans. Fumbling at her pockets, she realized that they were empty. Her phone, cigarettes, and lighter were gone as well as the small wallet she carried in her jeans pocket every day. She sighed, a flicker of anger stirring through her. Raising her eyes, she saw that a gray tumbler abruptly had appeared on the ledge next to her. Alarmed, she skittered away from it, saliva pooling in her mouth. She craved liquid. Cautiously, she scooted toward it, glancing about the room. How had the vessel suddenly appeared?

She smiled tremulously. This had to be a dream. That's all. She'd fallen asleep somewhere...in the truck? And this was her dream. Her very strange dream. She reached for the cup and saw that it was two-thirds full of water. Salivary glands twisted in her jaw as she lifted the clay-like cup to her lips.

Her hand stayed its upward motion as a visual flash raced through her brain. She saw Sage, blood gushing from one side of her mouth. Trembling, her hand lost its grip and the cup tumbled from her hands, smashing into small shards on the metal floor and spraying water halfway across the room.

Lily moaned and hung her face in her hands. Memory was creeping back and she remembered going to see the President... Uncally...Sage and Lanny. The water. There was something wrong with the water.

Another flash hit her and she recoiled. A small, dark blue vessel, a gash in its side. Faces peering at her, faces like owls, like ferrets, eyes beady and bright. Lily gasped and fell back on the ledge, feeling as though she might pass out. Then, suddenly, she did.

The heat was intense when next Lily came to her senses. She was gasping in the furnace that surrounded her. The room had darkened and she realized that she must be outside because dusky red light was now slanting dimly through the high slits. She sat slowly and saw that the broken cup had disappeared. Anger rose anew and she embraced it. It cleared her mind and she knew what had happened. Her tongue probed her dry mouth and she understood that she was probably going to die here. The alien Greys knew what she had done and this was her punishment for going against them.

Flynn. She looked around again and realized that the aliens must know how the IDBs traveled, hence the metal box sans any glass windows. Or glass surfaces. Or large openings of any kind. And the clay cup.

Tears pooled in her eyes as she faced the inevitability of her death. Sadness swamped her as she realized she would not be missed. Her mother was, no doubt, dead, her father already gone, and Sage dead or dying. She thought of Uncally, Diana, Tessie, and oddly, Hunter Moon, the airman from the plane who had warned her about protecting herself. She sighed and resolved that she wouldn't die easy. Why should she? This had not...none of it...been her choice. She leapt to her feet, swayed but steadied herself. With grim determination, she strode to the door and pounded it with both fists, putting her entire hundred thirty pounds into each blow.

"Let me out, you bastards," she screamed as loudly as her raspy, dry throat would allow. "You can't do this, you fuckers!"

She stopped, exhausted, some unrealized time later, and fell onto the floor, panting and sweaty. She felt as though she could die right then, the sound of her heart roaring in her ears. Closing her eyes, she drifted, reliving her life, until she drifted off, to sleep or unconsciousness, she didn't care.

CHAPTER TWENTY-TWO

The heavy clank of the door woke her, but the light hitting her in the face immediately slammed her eyes closed again. She forced them open, one hand shielding her face. She scrambled to stand, unwilling to meet her alien captors in such a vulnerable position.

The light swerved from her face and a man came into focus. A man, not an alien creature, though several small, naked, egg-headed creatures clustered near him.

Lily's lips curled in a weak sneer. "Major Nilsson. Didn't expect to see you here," she croaked.

Nilsson turned and shooed the alien creatures out with nods of reassurance. He closed the door, then turned back to Lily. He sighed and shook his head.

"I know this looks bad…"

"Duh," Lily barked. She moved to lean against one of the side walls, horrified to see that her hands were shaking. She clasped them together.

With another heavy sigh, Nilsson moved to place his flashlight on the metal ledge of the bed. He pressed the industrial light into lantern mode, then sat heavily, resting his chin in his palms. They remained in silence for many minutes.

"So, what did they promise you?" Lily asked finally. Feeling as though her legs couldn't hold her much longer, she slid down the wall and crouched at the bottom.

Nilsson sighed again. "The usual…plus staying alive when they take over."

"And you're okay with this?"

He slammed a palm against the metal deck and glared at her, his face a menacing shadow. "Of course not!"

"Then why?" she snapped angrily.

"You have no idea, little girl, how incredibly powerful these creatures are. We're like…like ants to them."

"So you simply give up, roll over, and say 'here's my world, have at it'?"

"Of course not," he stated again. "You negotiate. That's what I'm trying to do."

"What about the other ones, the IDBs. They've helped before."

He snorted loudly. "Oh, yes, the high and mighty IDBs."

Lily waited, then spread her hands at his persisting silence. "Yes! What about them? They want to help us."

"Oh, do they? You don't seem to understand. We're merely a toy to them. Earth people are simply dolls they play with—"

"But," she interjected. "They helped out with the flu, with other things, wars, threats—"

"For themselves, Miss Dawson. To preserve their toys, so they can continue to play."

Lily stared at Nilsson's bent, silhouetted figure. "I won't believe that," she said eventually. "The president—"

"Knows nothing," he shouted before she could finish. "He only knows the drivel his advisers feed him. No US president has ever had an original thought. Our government is a perpetual machine traveling the same worn path time and again while crap like this happens. He has no clue."

Silence fell again. A lengthy silence.

"And that makes it all okay," Lily whispered.

Nilsson cleared his throat. "They want you to contact your IDB."

"Why?"

"I don't know, Dawson, and I don't care," he answered wearily. "Just do what they say."

"Why should I?" she protested. "Why should I do anything for them?"

"Because you'll stay in here until you mummify. No one is coming for you and you can't drink the water anymore. You're in the middle of nowhere, and believe me, when that sun comes up tomorrow and the next... Well, it won't be cool and comfy."

Lily jutted out her chin, even though she knew he couldn't see details in the dimness. "I don't care."

He chuckled softly. "You will."

He stood and lifted the light. "I'll check on you tomorrow evening. Maybe you'll have reconsidered by then." He walked toward the door. "Remember, Miss Dawson, time isn't quite the same to them as it is to us. They'll wait you out. You'll see. And they'll simply find another way to get what they want."

Lily listened to the strange chittering sounds of communication coming from outside as she crawled to the ledge and hoisted herself onto it. Her mind tried to interpret what the major had told her, but somehow the ideas wouldn't gel in her tired brain. She was filled with horror, with terror... and with hopelessness. This is what her country, her world had degenerated into. Betrayal to a power far more insidious than any earthbound threat.

She lay on her side on the warm ledge, curled into a fetal coil, and allowed her thumb to tickle at her bottom lip, anticipatory to its entering her mouth. Here she would die.

She sighed deeply and shifted, lurching in alarm when something hard and cool touched her brow. She reared back, gasping in fear. Gingerly, she extended her hand, eyes squinting to peer into the darkness that had settled into the room again like a satanic quilt. Her fingers encountered something metallic. Wait, smooth like…like glass.

She eagerly grasped the object, using her fingers as eyes. Eyeglasses. Nilsson must have dropped them…or left them. Though she wanted so very badly to press her palm to the cool glass surface, her hand hesitated. Suppose this is what they wanted? For her to call Flynn this way? Tears born of frustration sprouted. She had to protect Flynn and its people, but what if what Nilsson said was true, that the IDBs really didn't care?

She thought of her journey to Washington. She thought of Flynn's concern when she…he…it had seen the news footage about the illness. She thought of Flynn's urgency and pressure to abide by this world's rules. As if unbidden, Lily's hand pressed firmly against the smooth, cool lens. "Flynn," she whispered. "Flynn."

Lily heard voices and metal clanging even as her mind filled with white light and heat seemed to cook her from the inside out. Her eyes felt as though they would explode from her skull and her mouth tingled and burned.

"I'm sure I dropped them here…" she heard Nilsson say, the rest of his words drowned out by the ringing of a loud alarm bell.

"Clear!" someone shouted as she passed into unconsciousness, awash in searing pain as she burned.

There was a cool cloth on her forehead and her hand was held in softness. A melodious, familiar voice soothed her.

"Sage?" she croaked. "I died, Sage. It was Nilsson…" she whispered as she started to go under again. Soft hands brushed her forehead and tears spilled from Lily. She sobbed. "It hurts," she muttered.

"I know, I know," someone whispered back. "It will pass."

"Pass, yes." Lily tried to smile but felt as though she had no lips. And smiling made the pain worse.

CHAPTER TWENTY-THREE

"Lily? Miss Dawson, we're going to move you now. Are you ready?"

Lily crept toward wakefulness, feeling compelled to respond for politeness' sake. She mumbled something.

Someone sighed and Lily felt hands touch her firmly. Her world rotated as searing pain inundated her. Unable to help herself, she screamed louder than she could ever remember screaming and shifted into eerie, immediate wakefulness. Her eyelids were stuck together, but the sudden wakening pried at them and she saw her surroundings through watery lenses.

"No! Stop!" she cried out, eyes weeping with indignation and her voice oddly muffled.

"I'm sorry, sweet girl, but we have to move you so you'll heal evenly," a kind, female voice said.

Cool mist, a light liquid, washed across her body, easing some of the pain almost immediately.

"Thank you, thank you..." she muttered gratefully as she wept.

Sleep was a welcome mother standing with open arms.

Sometime later the sound of humming roused her. There were several voices, both male and female, and they hummed together, finally breaking into a song. A song Lily knew. It was an Acoma song.

"Sage?" she croaked.

Her hand was taken, but she only felt the motion, not the flesh, the touch. "Here, little flower. I'm here."

Lily fought to open her eyes, wanting desperately to see the dear face from her childhood. Each movement wrought new agony, though, and she realized that she had been seriously hurt.

"Am I okay?" she ground out.

"You will be," Sage whispered. "Let the body heal."

Lily nodded as much as she was able. *Heal body*, she thought to herself before falling asleep again.

Her eyes flew open sometime later and she remembered important things. The Purge, her sick mother, Flynn, and saving the water. Had it been a dream? Though her eyes were open, she saw only faint light. Sounds penetrated. She heard purposeful steps on cushioned soles, muted voices from far away, faint beeps.

Hospital. She was in a hospital. She tried to think back, to remember what had happened to her and realized much of it was a blur. She remembered the smell of metal. Scary faces looming above her as she lay dazed on the hard ground. Non-human faces. She shuddered as she remembered them.

New waves of discomfort rippled through her. Movement wasn't painful, really, only uncomfortable. She needed to take stock of her condition. She moved her jaw and though it was stiff, it moved okay. She allowed her head to fall slowly to one side. No pain.

Through the dimness she could see that she was indeed in a hospital room. Lighted machines stood sentinel at the head of her bed and drawn curtains covered what was surely a window. Shaking with muscle fatigue, she moved her head back to center and then slowly down on the other side. A shadowed bed was on that side, a body buried under blankets, obviously asleep. So, she was sharing a room. She took a deep breath and part of her mind realized that there was something different about the other bed, but the thought wouldn't gel. She returned her head back to center.

Cautiously she moved her shoulder blades, then her upper arms to the elbows. Discomfort, stiffness but no real pain. She spread her fingers and pain radiated along her left arm. Ahh, maybe her fingers were broken. She couldn't see them because the arm was bound somehow, maybe under the coverlet. Her right hand seemed to be okay, but there was an odd stiffness and that arm was bound as well.

God, was she strapped to the bed? Panic sent a white-hot arc of heat through her body and adrenaline made her heart race. Immediately an alarm sounded and one of the machines shot beams of light throughout the darkened room. Rapid footsteps approached outside the room, but even as the door swung open, warm arms enveloped her upper body.

"Stay calm, Lily, stay calm," said a sleepy but familiar voice. "We're here. You're okay. You're okay."

Dim light filled the room and the alarm was switched off.

"She's okay," the voice said.

"Lily?" A face appeared before her, a kind but unfamiliar visage. "You're in the hospital, sweetie. In Albuquerque. Are you in pain?"

Lily shook her head in the negative, eyes blinking rapidly in the new light. "What…" she croaked, then swallowed deeply. "What happened?"

The familiar voice spoke again, and Hunter's face cleared into being above her. "You were in the desert, hon, and a kind hiker brought you here to the hospital. Do you remember that? He said his name was Flynn."

A meaningful look passed from Hunter's eyes to hers, and Lily remembered that secrecy was a large part of her life now.

"Yes, yes, I remember now," she whispered.

Hunter smiled and leaned to kiss Lily's bandaged brow. "I'm so glad you're okay," she whispered against that brow.

Lily nodded and the nurse leaned to adjust the oxygen cannula under her nose.

"You're a very lucky girl, Lily. Very lucky. Would you like some shaved ice?"

Lily nodded and the nurse patted her right hand. "I'll be right back."

After the door closed, Lily tilted her face toward Hunter. "How long?"

"A little more than twelve weeks," Hunter responded. "Flynn had to bring you through their world and you were pretty bad off by the time he was able to get you here."

"How...bad?"

Hunter patted her arm. "No need to worry about that now, Lily. You need to focus on healing."

Lily sighed. "How bad?" She realized suddenly that she couldn't feel her body below the waist. Was she paralyzed? She braced herself for the bad news.

Hunter hung her head. "You were exposed to a lot of radiation, Lily, but only briefly. Flynn wrapped you in energy but mostly it was your upper body."

"My legs? I can't feel them."

Hunter nodded and one thumb lovingly caressed the planes of Lily's cheekbone. "They've given you a block, in your spine. One leg was damaged badly and they're trying to save it."

Lily nodded, relieved. Maybe she wasn't paralyzed.

"My hand...my hand is hurt."

"Yes," Hunter said, her eyes darkening. "You lost a finger. They think it's frostbite, from exposure," she whispered. "Flynn told them you'd been out in the desert for several days."

"All right, Lily," the nurse announced as she reentered the room. "Here's some ice for you. Doctor Stepelen is on call tonight, and I've asked him to pop in and have a look at you."

The nurse, Marilyn J, according to her badge, pressed a button and raised the head of Lily's bed a foot or so. Lily slid to one side, disoriented, and Hunter caught her, recentering her on the bed.

"Thank you," Lily said weakly.

Hunter nodded and took the paper cup of ice and plastic spoon from the nurse. "I'll do that for you," she told Marilyn, smiling.

Marilyn smiled back. "You're such a help, Hunter, you really are."

Marilyn patted Lily's thigh, something Lily saw more than felt. "Your wife is a very good woman, Lily. You should cherish her."

Lily swung her eyes to Hunter, who blushed a startling shade of crimson. "Oh, I will. I do," Lily responded, unreleased laughter filling her and brightening her soul just a bit.

"Well, you two relax. I'll bring the doctor in as soon as he is free. Let the ice melt or chew it slowly, Lily. Your body hasn't had anything by mouth for quite some time." She nodded meaningfully at Hunter. "You ring the bell if you need me."

After she left, Hunter lifted a half spoonful of ice to Lily's lips. Lily hesitated. "Wait. Is the ice okay?" she asked.

Hunter nodded. "Yes, the water here is filtered and the system has been sterilized."

Lily accepted the offering, her eyes studying Hunter as she gently chewed and let the cool water pour along her parched throat.

"It was so I could be here all the time," Hunter explained finally, her eyes looking at the ice, then at Lily. "Colonel Collins suggested it."

A tense silence fell and Lily studied Hunter. "What aren't you telling me?"

Hunter took in a deep breath. "The baby is okay."

"The baby?" Lily wondered if she'd heard correctly.

"Yes, they used pain meds that aren't processed too heavily through the placental wall. They thought they'd have to abort several weeks ago, but the scan they did yesterday showed no physical harm. Blood tests were normal, as well."

"A baby?" A slow, garbled laugh emerged from Lily, and she groaned and leaned to one side. "Oh, God. Don't make me laugh, Hunter. It hurts."

Hunter watched Lily, a bewildered look on her features, and this set Lily off again.

"Lily! Stop! You're going to hurt yourself," Hunter warned.

Lily realized suddenly that she could no longer breathe air in and her eyes opened wide as alarms sounded by her ear. She fixed panicked eyes on Hunter and realized suddenly that if she was to die, this dear face could be the last face she would see. That was okay. Though terrified, she winked at Hunter and tried a tremulous smile. Hunter stared in wide-eyed terror, then leapt to her feet and raced around the bed. Darkness, Lily's old friend, came to her once again.

CHAPTER TWENTY-FOUR

"Gin! Ha!"

Hunter stared at her with wide eyes. "How do you *do* that? I think you're cheating. No one gets gin three times in a row."

"And with a wounded fin, no less," Lily responded, holding up her bandaged hand. "I can't even hold the cards." She indicated the plastic card holder that rested on the rolling hospital bed tray. "Thank you for this, by the way."

"You are very welcome, wife, but I still think you're cheating somehow."

"Nope, a good wife never cheats," she intoned with a wide-eyed, serious look.

Hunter studied Lily's face for a long beat. "You're looking good, Lily," she said finally. "You can hardly see the redness."

"That coconut oil concoction you and Sage came up with seems to be working." Lily lifted one hand and touched her pink cheek.

A soft knock sounded at the door and both women swiveled their faces toward the portal as a short man of East Indian descent entered.

"Doc Swami," Lily crowed gently. "How are you this morning?"

"Almost as good as you," Doctor Dwarka Mehta said with a beaming smile that lit his dark, shadowed eyes.

"Cool," Lily said, grinning. "Any idea when I can blow this Popsicle stand?"

Doctor Mehta clasped his hands behind his back and rocked on his heels a few times. "Well, I am thinking that maybe today would be a good day to lose the Popsicle stand," he replied. "If you are doing as good as the nurses tell me."

Lily turned an excited gaze to Hunter, who stood and rolled the table to one side.

"I take a look, yes?" Doctor Mehta asked, indicating her legs.

"Hell, yes," Lily cried, grabbing the thin blankets and tossing them off her legs.

The doctor moved closer, donning the glasses that had been hanging on a chain around his neck.

The three stared at the miracle that was Lily's lower body. After the radiation exposure, which had cooked Lily's legs like a microwave, from the inside out, the physicians had been forced to make a long vertical incision on each leg to allow the damaged tissues to expand and heal without tearing her flesh into ragged gashes. Now, dead tissue removed and healing flesh maintained, each incision had been sewn closed by the plastic surgery fellow. The legs, considering what they'd been through, looked pretty darned good.

Doctor Mehta pulled on gloves that he fetched from the box next to Lily's bed. "Well, let's see if we can remove this drain so you can go home."

He reached for Lily's left leg, the one most damaged, and gently manipulated the plastic drain protruding from the bottom of the incision, close to her ankle. He looked at Hunter. "Press the call button, please."

Hunter complied and Doctor Mehta, via intercom, asked the nurse to bring a suture kit. Moments later, Marilyn entered and Hunter packed up the playing cards so the medical personnel could use the table. Marilyn smiled at Lily as she laid the kit on the table. She pulled on gloves and opened it. "Looks like this is your lucky day, Ms. Lil. That nasty old tube just might be going away."

Mehta laughed as he reached for surgical scissors. "And she can go home if she promises to be a good girl," he said distractedly.

Lily watched in fascination as the doctor snipped a few stitches and gently waggled the drainage tube loose. There was surprisingly little pain, merely an itching sensation, and she let out the breath she'd been holding.

"There," Mehta said as he bent to examine the wound for infection. "I think this is healing nicely."

"Feels good," Lily said in a musing tone. Her hand absently caressed her rounded belly. Though only five months along, the baby had begun to kick often with sweet little flutterings.

Doctor Mehta retrieved a butterfly bandage from the kit and pulled the small opening together and fastened it. He laid a dressing on the butterfly and secured it with paper tape.

"This should heal together by the end of the week. If all still looks good, no redness, no draining, no tenderness or fever, you can come into the outpatient clinic downstairs and have the rest of the stitches removed then. The nurses will give you aftercare paperwork but you know not to soak in a tub or pool, keep it as dry as possible, and no more than thirty minutes..." He looked at her with a serious frown. "Thirty minutes *total* of standing or walking a day for the next four weeks. I mean this, Lily. Tell me you understand."

Lily nodded at him, her demeanor serious. "I do, doc. Thirty minutes each day, no more."

"These legs are continuing to heal on the inside too and you are very lucky to still have them." He looked at her over the top of his eyeglasses. "Very lucky," he reiterated.

Lily gulped, remembering in speedy flashes the past few months of pain and anguish as the medical team tried desperately to save them. "Yes, sir."

Mehta smiled, showing his small, crooked teeth and, surprisingly, a dimple in his right cheek. He held out his hand to Lily. "I suppose this is when we say good-bye. You have been a good, brave patient."

Fighting tears, her emotions once again all over the place, Lily took his hand and shook it gently. "Thank you for helping to save my legs, Doctor," she whispered.

Mehta removed his glasses and inclined his head. "Take very good care of yourself, Lily. Gain some weight. Eat for two like you mean it."

Marilyn grinned and gave Lily a thumbs-up sign as she collected the surgical kit and followed the doctor from the room.

Hunter sat on the side of the bed, so she could see Lily's face. "So, that's it, then. Back to the ranch you go."

"Hunter," Lily began slowly. "I can't even begin to thank you for being here with me…"

Hunter slowly pressed one finger to Lily's lips. "No, don't," she said.

"But—"

Hunter shook her head. "Nope. Listen, I'm going to call everyone, okay? You be okay for a few minutes?"

Lily nodded and watched as Hunter's short, slim form stepped from the room. Lily switched her attention to her legs, truly amazed to still have them. The ongoing physical therapy was grueling, but she did have use of both her legs and that thrilled her. She'd probably always need a cane, but she was oddly okay with that.

She lifted her left hand and studied it. The pinkie finger was missing down to the second knuckle but they had managed to preserve a small nub, saying it would make the hand more useful. The unbandaged ring finger next to it still had a few blisters and some discoloration from its time exposed in Flynn's dimension. Her eyes traveled up her arms, which had been surprisingly little scathed by the journey. Her face, shoulders, and chest, which Flynn had covered by a shield of energy, according to Hunter, were burned only slightly. Lily sighed as she thought about the astronomical hospital bill she would receive, but in all honesty, she was glad to be alive and away from the evil little gremlins who had kidnapped her.

But most intriguing was the baby growing in her womb. She had no idea how the pregnancy had happened. Flynn had visited her once, in his ranch hand guise, and explained—before she had asked—that the energy field had impregnated her. Biologically impossible, of course, and he'd had no explanation for how it had occurred. There was precedent, however, and several religious icons had been a merging of human and the energy collective.

"I'm having a little Jesus," she muttered aloud as she spread the blankets across her legs.

A lot had changed during her five months in the hospital. The people of the United States had survived, thanks to the IDBs, and the virus engineered by the Greys hadn't spread beyond the borders. The Polar Purge had left a lot of damage behind, however. It attacked the circulatory system by filling the blood with a type of ash that coagulated it. Many survivors had lost limbs to the resultant gangrene-type reactions. Others suffered suffocation or dementia requiring full-time care. Almost two million had died.

It could have been a lot worse.

Lily sighed and looked out the window. It opened onto a graveled rooftop that connected to an adjoining building, and Lily had delighted in watching the doves form their little social groups there. Today only two were home, Blackbeak and Maisie. They huddled together in the morning chill as if waiting for the sun to finish warming them.

"Well, Sage said that since you'll be coming home, she won't make the trek in today. She's gonna get everything ready for you," Hunter announced as she reentered the room.

"I sure hope that doesn't include installing a hospital bed," Lily said, slapping the rails of the bed. "Ugh!"

Hunter laughed and tucked her cell phone into her pocket. "I dunno. Seems to suit you these days."

Lily pulled an indignant face and chucked a pillow at Hunter. She ducked and the pillow took out a vase of flowers on the ledge behind her. Hunter turned and studied Lily with wide eyes. "Now look what you've done," she scolded, murmuring to herself as she moved to mop up the water and right the flowers.

Lily sighed, swept the covers aside and swung her legs as one unit over the side of the bed. She hoisted herself upright and grimaced as she reached for her walker. "I think I'll get dressed," she told Hunter as she tottered to the closet.

"Here, let me help you with that," Hunter said, gently inserting herself between Lily and the closet. "Do the words 'badger-headed' mean anything to you?"

Lily chuckled and maneuvered backward. "Yeah, that's the new Native name you and Sage have bestowed upon me."

"Exactly right." Hunter pulled clothing from the closet and moved to the bed. "I'm not sure about the shoes, Lil," she said thoughtfully. "But the yoga pants should be soft enough."

Lily moved toward the clothing, her left leg beginning to throb. "I can just wear those hospital sock thingies home."

"You need some help?" Hunter asked, hovering nervously.

The throbbing was making Lily testy, so she only shook her head, biting her bottom lip. She turned so she was sitting on the bed and reached for her shirt.

Hunter moved behind her and turned toward the window as Lily removed her pajama shirt and pulled on a sweatshirt. She'd lost a lot of weight that she really couldn't afford to lose and the shirt hung loosely, even over her rounded abdomen. Shirted, she had to rest a moment and catch her breath. She leaned her head to one side, resting it on her shoulder. Suddenly, Hunter was in front of her.

"Come on, Lil," she said quietly. "Cut yourself some slack, why dontcha? Plus, maybe you could give a girl a thrill."

Lily smiled as Hunter lifted the yoga pants and slipped them over Lily's feet, working them gently up over the stitched and bandaged legs. She wrapped her arms about Lily and held her upright as she slipped the pants over her bottom. She lingered there before carefully releasing Lily back onto the bed and stepping away.

Lily, panting, eyed Hunter with squinted eyes. "So, was it good for you?"

Hunter laughed as she began gathering Lily's possessions. Lily watched her, trying to breathe slowly and deeply. She felt as weak as a newborn puppy and hoped that it would pass soon. Maybe being home, out in the fresh air and sunshine, would help. Home. She blinked her eyes rapidly. Home. She realized suddenly that the ranch was now her home. Unless...she wondered what had ever happened with Nilsson.

"Hey, Hunter. What ever happened with that snake Nilsson?"

Hunter moved to the easy chair and took a seat. "Ah, I was wondering when you'd ask about him. It was treason, pure and simple. Last week he was stripped of rank and convicted of third degree treason—seditious conspiracy."

"And that means..."

"Well, it's a capital offense."

"And that means..."

"Lily, you don't need to worry about this..."

"Death. He'll be put to death."

Hunter sighed. "Lily—"

"I'm glad," she said quietly. "What he did was wrong. He was gonna turn us over to the little bastards, without a second thought. He deserves to die for that." She pressed her mouth into a grim line.

Hunter sighed again as she glanced toward the open door. "It won't happen right away. He'll be jailed for a time because he confessed, and his defense is lobbying for lifetime incarceration. Let's not talk about this here."

Lily lay back on the bed and Hunter moved to help lift her legs onto the mattress. "They're throbbing a little," she admitted.

"It'll take time," Hunter said softly. "Let the body heal on its own time," she added.

Lily grinned. "Yeah, that's what Sage told me."

"A wise woman."

"So, Lily. Going home." TomTom Lawry was suddenly standing at the foot of her bed.

"Sheesh. Sneak around much?" Lily responded.

TomTom smirked at her. "You need to pay better attention, paleface."

TomTom, her physical therapist, had been torturing Lily on a daily basis for the past two weeks. She had to give him some credit. At least she was upright and mobile. It didn't mean she had to let him know that, though. "So, are you here to torture me as a going away present? I can tell you right now, I am so not in the mood."

TomTom crossed his arms, the movement causing his long, ebony ponytail to slither behind his shoulder. "Are you ever?" he asked with a nonchalant wave of one hand.

Hunter grinned but ducked her head when Lily gave her the look.

"Actually, you will be happy to learn, I *am* cutting you loose." He waved a sheaf of paper at her. "You will have to do these stretches every day, though, or I'll bring your butt back here so fast it'll make your head spin."

Lily squinted at Hunter, then at TomTom. "And I'm sure you have spies in place to make sure I do them, don't you?" she accused.

TomTom laughed and handed the papers to Hunter. "Wouldn't you like to know, for sure?" he asked. "Make sure you stop if you feel real pain, but I still want you to push the limits a little, like you did here," he instructed. "My card's on top and you call or email if you have any questions."

He moved around the side of the bed and raised her pants legs. He examined the incisions and manipulated her feet, testing for flexibility. "How much activity did the doctor say?"

"Thirty minutes, tops," Hunter answered, ignoring Lily's arch glance.

"Okay, so no more than ten minutes of stretching when you wake up, still in bed, then ten middle of the day while upright, then ten at night in bed. Got it?" His dark brown eyes bored into Lily's.

"Jawohl, boss." Lily saluted and smiled sweetly.

TomTom grimaced at her, as if disgusted, or unbearably tolerant. "So, boy or girl?" He indicated her baby bump.

"No idea. The hospital knows, but I wanted a surprise."

He nodded and fell silent.

"You did well," he said finally. Seriously. "It was good to see your progress."

Lily nodded, tears sprouting. "Thank you for being such a monster," she said.

"It's what I do," TomTom said. He held his hand out for a knuckle bump, which Lily returned. "Take care of yourself, paleface."

"You too, Indian boy," Lily whispered.

CHAPTER TWENTY-FIVE

"You didn't have to do all this, Saysay," Lily said as she shifted her bony bottom in the wheelchair. "I know you are still recovering, yourself."

"That was long ago," Sage replied, brushing off Lily's concern.

"Here you go, Lil," Margie said, handing Lily a soda.

Lily accepted gratefully, then lifted her glass in a toast to Sage and Margie. "To good friends, to family," she said softly. The fizzy sweetness of the soda washed across her tongue and tears sprouted. Once again, her emotions had been all over the place, thanks to the pregnancy, and seeing a house full of people welcoming her home had touched her deeply.

"You know, Lily. You spent mosta your childhood here, in the desert. You know this place like the back of your hand," Margie said, staring out across that desert. "How you could come to get lost is just beyond me."

Lily nodded in agreement, hating the lies that she must live her life under now. "I got turned around. I was so upset by Sage being sick, I don't think I was thinking clearly. Should never have left the truck. Stupid move."

"Yeah, and you pregnant. Why on earth didn't you tell us?" Margie took her seat and patted Lily's leg.

Sage nodded, as if in agreement, her good hand rubbing the numb one obsessively. It was a new habit, since the Purge. That and the smell of hot red pepper and rosemary cream that preceded Sage when she entered a room. It was as though rubbing it would bring back feeling. At least she'd been able to keep the hand. Many of the Purge's victims had not.

About the lies… Lily remembered a particular journal entry in which her father had agonized about that same issue. It was a shame that the world they lived in prevented honesty. Whether from fear of them becoming terrified or possibly finding an exploitive way to profit, humans simply could not be told the truth. A sad but true fact.

Her father's journal had been a constant companion as she'd healed. She'd yet to tell anyone else about it, even Hunter or Collins, feeling that it was the one truly personal connection her father had forged with her. Even though she'd read the entire journal, more than twenty years' worth, she still went back and read random sections from time to time. She had a much better understanding of the IDBs' importance to national and global security now. And she realized that the governmental powers that be were, and had to remain, mostly clueless to much of the IDB and Grey presence. As her father pointed out, the president and his cabinet were only human and were subject to human frailty, a luxury that her father and now Lily, could not embrace. Did it make her less than human? No, she preferred to think of it as uber-human. She had progressed, via the meager experiences that she'd already had, past the human experience.

Reading the journals had also allowed her to get to know her father anew at each rereading, a true blessing. She'd seen again the random, silly sense of humor he'd possessed. She had forgotten about that after dealing with her mother's rancor toward him.

She realized suddenly that her name had been called and that a loud humming sound had filled the room. Alarmed, she rose on wobbly legs, and Sage hurried to steady her. "What is that?" she cried out.

She heard a new, accelerating noise and realized Hawkeye was keening softly and rocking from foot to foot. One of his hands reached out and caught on the streamers hanging from Lily's welcome home banner and a pink crepe paper ribbon floated down onto his dark hair. His quiet, stocky mother moved closer and calmed him with soothing gestures.

Lanny, standing next to Hawk and his family, spoke softly to them, then spoke loudly to the twenty or so people gathered. "Just a helicopter. That's all. It's landing outside."

A mad rush of people reached Lanny's side and stared out the large bay window. Lily saw the grayish, insectile body of the vehicle as it blocked daylight, the whirring blades of the propeller creating a mirage of solidity. Lily took a deep breath, realizing it had to be Collins. She'd been surprised by his long, periodic absences during her extensive hospitalization but knew that the crisis, even six or seven months after the release of the viral threat, was still winding down and needed his involvement.

The window was too high for her to see Collins deplane, but the helicopter rose and arched away from the house, the compression of the blades jarring the floor and causing the sensation of a mild earthquake. Lanny approached the door and opened it before anyone could knock. To Lily's surprise, Tess rushed into the room, a brightly colored present in her hand. She was glancing back, eyes wide, but turned and caught Lily's gaze. She mouthed something as she moved closer, but Lily didn't catch it. She lowered herself back into the chair as Tess reached her.

"What the hell is going on?" Tess asked.

Lily shrugged. "I'm not sure, hon. I just work here."

Tess stepped to one side and they watched the hallway together. Heavy footsteps sounded and two larger-than-life men entered. One was Collins, in air force camouflage, and the other was a suit with dark, straight hair, and thick-rimmed eyeglasses.

Collins was conversing with Lanny and the suit was studying the living room and the crowd of people—farmhands, neighbors, and old and new friends who had gathered to welcome Lily home. His eyes rested on Lily and his face brightened. Suddenly, Hunter, who'd been off to one side talking with ranch hand Lunan Dix, moved protectively to Lily's side.

The man approached Lily. He paused and removed his glasses, going through an elaborate process of removing a cleaning cloth from a protective plastic sleeve, cleaning the lenses, then refolding and replacing the cloth, before finishing his approach. Glasses reseated, he regarded Lily with smiling eyes and a boyish grin.

"Miss Dawson?" he queried, extending his right hand, his eyes dropping to her belly. "My name is Wendell Ames. It's good to finally meet you in the flesh, so to speak." He smiled, as if lauding his own cleverness.

"Well, Wendell," Lily said, taking his hand and shaking it firmly. "It's very good to finally see the face on the other side of our texts."

"Yes, ma'am," he agreed. "I was very glad when you told us about your successful recovery. The desert can be a brutal enemy, now, can't it?"

"Indeed," Lily agreed. "And I am very glad to be alive today."

"I'm glad as well," Collins chimed in as he reached their side. He smiled and shook Hunter's hand, nodding in greeting, then kissed Lily's forehead. "You gotta be a lot more careful, Little Lil. You've got a little one to think about now."

Lily gave him an arch look accompanied by a mouth twisted in doubt. He laughed and raised both hands in surrender. "I know, I know."

"Wendell, Uncle Alan, these are my friends. Hunter and Sage, you know, but this is Tess who runs a restaurant in town, and then Lunan and Margie who work the ranch..."

The others pressed forward and began introducing themselves. "We're all ranch workers, mostly," Click said as he shook Wendell's hand.

"Speak for yourself," Cibola Rodriguez said as she elbowed him aside. "I'm Cibola, Sage and Lanny's daughter. I stay as far away from ranch work as I can."

"She speaks truth there," Lanny piped up, causing Sibby to titter with amusement. Her youngest son, Manuel, moved closer and grasped her thigh protectively. She pressed one palm to his short, jet hair as if reassuring him.

"There's food and soda here on the table. And iced tea," Lily said, gesturing toward the long table that had been set up in the family room.

"Wow," Collins exclaimed, making his way over to it. "Look at this spread."

Wendell grinned in his direction, then returned his attention to Lily.

"Miss Dawson, do you think we could speak privately for a few minutes?"

Lily was bewildered but curious. "Absolutely. Let's...ahh... let's go to Father's study."

She slowly, awkwardly rolled her chair along the hallway and into the study. It was unchanged but no longer creeped her out quite as much. Her father's journal had certainly changed her outlook on nearly everything.

"May I sit here?" Wendell asked, indicating an overstuffed leather chair situated in front of the hearth. His gaze flew to the glass statue on the desk.

"Certainly." Lily moved her wheelchair closer to that chair as Wendell sat.

He watched her briefly before clearing his throat and opening the leather satchel he carried. "Well, Miss Lil...may I call you that? Miss Lil?"

Lily nodded and tilted her head to one side, watching him.

"Well, Miss Lil. David, Mr. President, has asked me to come and offer you a job."

"A job?" Lily shifted in the chair. "What kind of job?"

He nodded as if he'd expected the question. "Officially the title is Civilian Liaison for International Security and you'd be under the envoy of Homeland Security but answerable only to the president. Via me, of course."

Lily grinned. "Of course." She grew somber as she mulled the proposition.

"It'll be what you are doing now, serving as the conduit. Or consultant, if you prefer. It's what your father did," he added quietly. "David trusts you without preamble, for some odd reason. Maybe because the, um, helpers do. Reason enough, I suppose."

He smiled at her, eyes gentle.

"Would I be paid?" Lily asked finally.

"Of course. Level three. Not as much as your father but enough to live well. I see you will soon have a child to take care of."

"Yes. And I will be a single mother, so I'm grateful to be able to work from the ranch here as I raise him or her."

Wendell nodded. "Yes. The job isn't too demanding, but it can be intense, even dangerous at times, as you no doubt realize. So, the father isn't…?"

"No. The father won't be involved," she said quietly, even as she wondered if this were true.

"Will your housekeeping staff remain here? As backup for child care should you need to leave suddenly?" he asked.

"Yes, of course. They are like family to me." Lily's voice changed to a musing tone. "You know, I just fell into this. It certainly wasn't what I had planned for my life."

She paused and took a deep breath. "I guess I didn't really have much of anything planned." She thought of her mother and the RV park in Florida and her heart lurched painfully.

Wendell continued to study her. "Sometimes when life gives you lemons, you just squeeze out what you can and make you some lemonade."

Lily turned to him and laughed. "Oh, my God," she moaned.

Wendell laughed with her. "Yes, I said it."

"So, you'll do it?" he asked finally when the levity had passed.

Lily shrugged. "Sure. Yes. I'm the one they chose."

"And you do realize that you will be bound by military code? If it can be proven that you leaked secure information to anyone not vetted by us, you will be subject to the strictest laws, the Congressional Code of Military Criminal Law, for treason."

Lily sighed. "Yes, yes, I fully understand. Just show me where to sign."

"I thought you'd never ask," he replied with a wide grin. He reached into the satchel and pulled out a stack of papers.

"Wait. What will I tell people? That I do, I mean."

"Your father had a substantial life insurance policy. That all comes to you now. I guess you don't have to tell anyone anything. You're a cattle rancher...like your father was." He smirked at her expectantly.

Lily nodded. "I guess I'll take up ranching, after all," she agreed. "Does Uncally...Colonel Collins know all the details now?"

Wendell nodded and rose to spread the eight contracts on the desk. "Yes, and Airman Moon knows a little of it. They've signed some of the same agreements that you'll need to sign."

"Anyone else?" She reached for her father's pen, wondering if he'd used it for much the same task.

"No. No one else. And it must stay that way," Wendell replied, his mouth in a firm line.

CHAPTER TWENTY-SIX

"So, what did the government want with you?" Hunter asked some time later.

Most of the guests had cleared out and, exhausted, Lily was sitting on the front porch with Hunter in the chair next to her. They were watching the rosy sky saying good night to the sun. Lily's hands had taken up their habitual stance atop her rounded abdomen and she was gently soothing the active child within.

"Just to talk about my father's life insurance policy," she replied, hoping it wasn't a lie really, merely a sin of omission. "And they told me that the government is picking up my hospital tab. You know, for helping save America and all."

"Woot!" Hunter whistled. "You made out like a bandit."

They sat in silence for some time, each lost in thought. Finally, Hunter cleared her throat. "Listen, is it okay if I wait until Saturday next week to clear out my stuff from the guest room? My roommate decided to sublet to make the rent and then...well, you won't believe it." She chuckled and her eyes shone in the sunset rainbow. "They fell in love. Mandy and the new guy who moved in with her."

Lily laughed and leaned her head back. "Where will you live now? You guys were on base, right?"

"Well, we were...I was, but, Stephen, a friend from school, says I can live in his grandfather's house outside Albuquerque. It's an old house and small, but he's only charging me two hundred a month."

"That's a sweet deal." Lily took Hunter's hand, surprising them, both. "Wish you could stay here. I don't want to be alone. I...I've never had a baby."

Hunter studied Lily. "You'd want that? Truthfully?"

Lily nodded and their eyes met, communicating eons of need and caring. "What about the father, Lil. Can you mend things with him?"

Lily sighed deeply and released Hunter's hand. She felt it was important that no one know about her child's strange inception. She wanted him, or her, to have as normal a life as possible.

"No. It's just me on this one. It's better that way."

Hunter nodded. "Well, you've got the Kya'nahs here and I'll come around on the weekends. Will that be okay? I love this ranch."

Lily grinned. "Well, yeah. Who will I beat at gin rummy if you're not around?"

Hunter laughed. "I'll only be an hour away so I can come visit regularly to tromp *your* ass."

"We never talked about your career, Hunter. Somehow we missed it during the months I was partially unconscious."

Hunter shrugged. "The usual. Airman basic in San Antonio, then two years in training. I'm almost done. Oh, it's medical, by the way. I used your hospital time as my inservice."

Lily squinted at her. "Well, how fortunate for you. Glad I could help out."

"Me too," Hunter responded flippantly, with a teasing grin. "Wanna hear the good part?"

Lily cocked her head.

"I've already got a job. With the VA hospital in Albuquerque. I'll start off as a Med Tech One, but there's plenty of room for advancement and bennies if I want to go to medical school."

"Oh, my God," Lily cried out. "That is so fantastic."

"Yeah, yeah, it is," she said.

They sat in silence as the night descended and cloaked them in dusk.

"What was it like?" Hunter asked finally.

"What?"

"Going into that other dimension. With Flynn."

Lily thought a moment. "Quiet. Really quiet and super bright. I think sometimes the sound of a million suns sounds like nothing at all," she whispered.

"Wow," Hunter responded. "I'm really glad you didn't die."

Lily nodded. "They offered me a job and I took it. Working with the IDBs. Like my father." The relief she felt in sharing with Hunter was almost palpable.

Hunter fixed a studying gaze on Lily. "I won't tell. You know that, right?"

Lily nodded. "I'm just a rancher."

Hunter grinned and sat back into the rocker.

Sage's shambling gait sounded in the hallway behind them.

"That's a lot of food," she said as she and Sibby stepped onto the porch. "I filled the main fridge and even moved some into the overflow one in the garage."

"You didn't expect people to bring stuff. You never do," Sibby retorted as she relaxed into one of the porch chairs, a big sigh of relief heralding her descent. "I told you not to have us make so much."

Sage sat in her usual rocking chair and began massaging her hand. "Guess I should have listened to all you younger ones."

"You never do," Sibby repeated. "Never have."

Sage only grunted in reply. She cocked her head sideways as if listening to the night.

"So, Hunter, what's next for you?" Sibby said as she kicked off her sneakers, the shoes making two loud, echoing thunks as they hit the porch floorboards.

"Back to base this weekend to finish up. Then on to the VA in the city."

"The Raymond Murphy?" Sibby queried.

"The very one."

Sibby sat back and folded one leg beneath her bottom. "Man, someone was looking out for you."

Hunter muttered in the affirmative.

"If it was me, though," Sibby continued. "I think I'd wanna get the hell outta here. Go somewhere new…different. You know?"

Hunter nodded. "You have family here, though. And now you have a husband and kids."

"Yeah, yeah, I know. As for Mom and Dad, I know they'd always have a home here for me. I meant if I was still young and single. Like you. Also, you're military, you could put in to go just about anywhere."

Hunter's grin could be heard in her voice. "Sounds to me like you're regretting not going into the force with me. I told you not to marry your sweetheart from school. But did you listen to me? Oh, no."

"No time for regrets," Sage intoned quietly.

"You've got family here, too," Sibby told Hunter.

"Yeah, I have lots of reasons to stay in the area," Hunter replied.

Lilly wondered at the warmth in Hunter's voice. Was it directed toward her? She hoped so.

Silence fell as each woman became lost in private thought.

"Do you think Mama would mind being buried next to Dad?" Lily asked finally.

Sage sighed. "Only you can know that," she replied.

"But what do you think?" Lily persisted.

"I think she'd wanna be wherever you are," Sibby interjected. "Seems logical. You are gonna stay here, right?"

Lily hesitated, thinking about it anew. Nope, no place she'd rather be. Her work was here now, as well. "Yep, plan to."

"Your mother came to love the ranch," Sage said. "This I know. I know how much it hurt her to leave."

"I think so, too," Lily agreed. "She tried to pretend otherwise because she was so angry when she left."

"The cemetery here is very pretty," Hunter offered quietly.

Lily sighed deeply. "Yeah, I think I'll bury her ashes there. I thought about putting her in the water off Florida but, well, I don't think her heart is there. It never was. I'm just sorry she had to die there."

"It was good of you to recommend that nurse as the new manager," Hunter said.

"Well, I think Lucy'll do a good job. She has a good head on her shoulders."

And she survived, Lily thought to herself. There's that.

"We've all lost a lot," Sage murmured, as if reading Lily's thoughts.

"Mama?" A young voice called from one side of the porch.

"Up here, Arturo," Sibby called out. "Is Manuel with you?"

"He fell asleep on Grandpa's sofa and Papa sent me to find you," Arturo said as he mounted the wide porch steps.

"Guess that means it's time to head home," Sibby said.

"Thank you for coming out," Lily said as she peered through the dusk and watched Sibby wriggle her feet back into her shoes.

"I can't say how good it is to see you, Lil. I'm sorry things have been so bad lately. Thank goodness our little pueblo all survived this plague," Sibby said as she stood and approached Lily. She leaned and pressed her cheek to Lily's. "Love you, sis. You take it easy, okay? You gotta take care of that little one cooking in you."

"I will," Lily said as her hand strayed back to her belly.

"And I sure hope you've learned that you can't fuck with the desert and win. You just can't," she added archly.

"Cibola! Little ears!" Sage scolded in a harsh hiss.

Sibby laughed as she straightened her back. "Yes, Mama, I hear you. Come on, let's get you home. You ready?"

Sage stood as Arturo took her arm. "Lily, you be okay getting to bed on your own?"

"I'll help her, Auntie," Hunter offered. "Go on home and don't you worry."

Sage moved to Hunter and squeezed her shoulder then patted Lily's cheek. "Be careful, girls, and call me if you need anything. Lanny can get me here in a minute."

"Thank you, Saysay. Good night," Lily told her, squeezing her good hand.

CHAPTER TWENTY-SEVEN

The change in the room's energy alerted her to Flynn's presence. No longer fearing the LDB, Lily moved slowly toward wakefulness. She stretched her stiff legs under the light blankets, then opened her eyes. Twit, who was sleeping on her legs, expressed disapproval of the late-night disturbance by digging in her claws. Lily yelped and the cat moved reluctantly to one side, eyes fixed on Flynn. Raising up and looking toward the chair, Lily saw Flynn waiting patiently, glowing hands clasped in front of the silver pajama set it wore.

"Hey, there," Lily said, yawning. "We really need to talk about our work hours." She switched on the bedside lamp. "Can you meet during business hours? Or is that not part of the deal?"

Flynn studied her blankly for a few seconds before catching on. "Ah, yes." It cocked its head, obviously conferring with the collective. "The duck said there was…less chance of…discovery here after your mother left, than in the office. He said he was not a…sleeper. And we offer compliments… We are…happy that we will be…working with you."

Lily conferred with her own inner collective. She supposed it *was* better this way. No lights for Sage and Lanny to notice as their cottage was on the other side of the house. "I think you mean congratulations," Lily said as she carefully adjusted her position. "Thank you. I want to also thank you again for saving me."

"We are sorry you were…hurt," Flynn said quietly.

"You did the right thing—what you had to do to get me away. I do not regret the injuries."

"Was the man punished properly? He will not be…put to death, we discovered." Flynn sighed and leaned back. "The Greys have…scattered for the time being."

Lily grimaced. "I am sorry to hear that he won't die. That sorry sack of shit needs to die so his stupidness will die with him."

Flynn watched her curiously. "So there is no…merit… there?"

"I don't know," Lily sighed. "I'm just angry at him for putting our nation, hell, our planet, in danger."

"And you," Flynn added.

"Yes, me," Lily agreed. "And many more. How many died, Flynn?"

"Two million, six hundred and forty-four thousand of your people. And some animals," Flynn replied. "Although the virus was not…engineered to harm animal…blood."

"It might not have been that high if he hadn't interfered."

Flynn shrugged in a very human manner and Lily laughed.

"I remember some of your world," she said. "Although I'm not sure world would be the right word. How do you exist in the coldness of space and the heat of the sun at the same time? With radiation thrown in for good measure? Also, what was that shifting thing, like shuffling a deck of cards?"

"We are energy," Flynn explained. "We are what your kind came from and what you will become again eventually. Matter is matter."

"You mean like after we die?"

"No," Flynn answered, shaking its head. "Your death is... too new...you and your...people will...die many, many times before you become energy such as we are."

"So, we don't go back to energy when we die? I thought we did."

"My people are...old...before your time existed. And very... different, though we were once very like you. Death for your people is...birds. Birds are closest."

Lily was bewildered and she wrinkled her nose in confusion. "Birds?" she repeated.

Flynn spread its hands and frowned. "Birds. Yes. Wings of motion...until there are no more."

Lily pondered this idea. "My father talked about the age of your people in his journal. He did research and believed that you may have seeded our planet. Created us."

Flynn nodded, silvery eyes fixing on Lily. "Yes...an accident when we collided. The type of life here was—"

"Primitive, before dinosaurs even, I know," Lily interjected. "I guess we *all* owe a lot to you."

"How are you...healing?" Flynn abruptly changed the subject.

Lily pulled the covers aside and Flynn rose to view her legs, leaning forward with its hands clasped behind its back. The familiar hum of energy shook Lily. The baby leapt into action, kicking and twisting deep within her.

"They will heal well," it said reassuringly as its gaze moved toward Lily's belly.

"Yes, they are doing well."

"Will you miss that part?" It indicated the missing fingertip. Lily shrugged. "It will be fine. It will have to be."

They fell into a prolonged silence and Lily wondered what common ground—other than saving the world—the two of them shared.

"So, I guess I won't see you again? Until we need you, I mean."

Flynn studied her, head characteristically cocked to one side. "We are friends...Little Lil. I am here for you anytime you need me."

"Use the glass statues? The ones here and in the office?"

"Yes, call us through any glass. Any...time you want."

"Can you meet my friend Hunter? Or anyone else? In another form, of course."

Flynn's lips pressed together and its shimmer increased. "No, your leader only allows one contact...it is the...law we agreed to."

Lily nodded and tears welled in her eyes. Fatigue swamped her. "I feel like I'm going to be all alone," she whispered. "That I will miss you."

Flynn's face softened and something very like emotion seated itself there. "We will never be far, Lily. We are your friend."

Lily hated her weakness and hated the yawn that suddenly overtook her.

"May we stay while you sleep?" Flynn asked. "We still don't...understand human rest. Are...curious."

Lily laughed shortly and pulled the blankets close as Flynn returned to the easy chair. After turning off the lamp, she glanced toward Flynn, whose yellow glow of energy brightened the entire room. She felt comforted, protected by the IDB's presence.

"Will the baby be a mix of both of us, Flynn?" she asked sleepily. "I mean, will he or she be human?"

"We believe so. There could be many...variances, but the baby will want to appear in your form."

"I'm glad. Life could be difficult for it, otherwise."

"She is very aware of you and has our extensive knowledge, our memories, even now. She will be...different."

"She? Will she have a static gender? I've been wondering..." Lily yawned once again but tried to stifle it with one palm.

"Gender is a human...paradigm but yes, she will be so."

Lily cradled her abdomen in both arms. "A little girl," she whispered.

"Yes. We call her Aili as she is part of our collective. Sleep now, Lil. We are here and you are...safe."

CHAPTER TWENTY-EIGHT

Lily soon settled into her new life at the ranch. She spent part of each day in her father's office, sorting through the ranch records until she had some idea of how it all worked. Near as she could see, cattle were sold at auction once or twice a year, and her father had kept impeccable records of which ones were sold and/or acquired at each auction. He had also kept an accounting of each calf born on the ranch. Although little had been entered since his death, a quick conversation with Lanny had produced a stained and tattered list, barely legible in pencil, that he had kept since her father's passing. It cited the birthdates and number tags of each new or sold animal. Lily diligently entered them into the paper ledger in the office, then sent the ledger to Margie, who entered it into a computerized spreadsheet.

Lily enjoyed the fact that her father had still used the oversized paper ledger book. She could almost feel his presence when she ran her hand across the smooth, cross-hatched pages.

She also realized that the household account that Sage, Lanny, and sometimes Margie used for regular household purchases was at rock bottom, and she was sure the two had been using some of their own money for groceries and feed. No matter what type of persuasion she tried, they would not allow her to reimburse them, but she quickly transferred money and set up auto payments into that account to keep it well-stocked.

Lucy, at the RV park in Florida, had packed up all their belongings and shipped them to Lily in New Mexico. She had included her mother's ashes and Lily had interred them next to her father. She liked having them together and visited them at least every other day, just to chat and to bolster a habit of visitation that she would share with her child, their grandchild, after she was born. She wondered how they would have accepted this mixing of human and collective in Aili but eventually decided that her father, at least, would have been pleased.

Hunter remained in the guest room, driving the sixty miles of highway each morning and evening to go to work at the VA hospital. Lily never questioned it, knowing that the bond they were forging a little each day would continue to keep them together. Hunter moving away for her medical school residency was something they never talked about, but it loomed like darkness.

"A new calf was born this morning," Hunter said one late summer day as they finished lunch. "Lunan let me catch it."

"Way cool," Lily responded, laying her napkin across her plate.

Sage had cooked a ham the day before and had made sandwiches and potato salad for their lunch.

"I thought calves were born in the spring," Hunter continued. "Fall's coming. Will the little heifer be okay?"

Lily rose and, leaning heavily on her cane, fetched the pitcher of iced tea. She topped off their glasses. "Yeah, I think so. You know how winters are here. Unpredictable as hell. We barn them up if the weather gets too bad. And Lanny likes to leave the bulls in with the dams so the births are spread out. He says it makes them all happier."

Hunter lifted an eyebrow as Lily sat heavily. Lily just grinned at her.

Hunter looked delicious. In uniform, she was amazing, but like this, in jeans, boots, and an old V-necked T-shirt, her tawny muscled arms exposed…well, it made Lily's breath catch in her throat.

As if sensing Lily's thoughts, Hunter shoved her mostly empty plate to one side and rested her arm on the table, the open hand beckoning. Lily took that hand and intertwined their fingers. She studied the hands.

"Do you know how much you mean to me?" Hunter whispered.

"You mean everything to me," Lily replied.

"So, what is this? This thing between you and me?" Hunter's thumb smoothed across their fingers.

Lily shrugged. "It is what it is. And I want more of it," she replied.

Hunter let go of Lily's hand and moved around the table to kneel next to Lily. Her palm pressed against the rounded belly and the baby rolled bodily, making Lily gasp and clutch at it.

"Wow!" she said, laughing. "Guess she likes you."

Hunter looked up at her, her gaze serious. "I don't know who the father is, I don't care," she said. "But will you let me be her other mother? Can we raise her together?"

"That's quite a commitment. Are you sure?" Lily bit her bottom lip in doubt.

"You're a package deal," Hunter said, laying her dark head against Lily's baby bump. "And I want to be with you, always. I love you."

Lily caressed the black, fragrant hair. She sighed. How did they come to this place? How did this odd series of miracles bring such love into her life?

"Marry me after she's born?" Lily asked.

Hunter stilled then finally looked up, her loving gaze finding Lily's. "Of course."

She paused and a huge smile creased her face. "You know, everyone at the hospital thinks we're already married."

Lily laughed. "Maybe we are," she said.

"Yes. I think we are," Hunter agreed.

Lily leaned forward, and they shared their first real kiss. Hunter's lips were warm and firm, her skin like velvet against Lily's cheeks. The baby kicked out suddenly as though pushing them apart, and the two women burst into helpless laughter, Hunter falling onto the floor.

"She's gonna be a soccer player," Hunter said after picking herself up and dusting off her jeans.

"She'll be a lot of things," Lily whispered.

Hunter bent and leaned her forearms on the table so she could better see Lily's face. "What's that?"

Lily bolstered herself and took Hunter's face in both hands. "The baby, Aili. She's Flynn's. Well, the collective's. It happened when they rescued me in the desert. I…I'm not sure how."

Hunter's face fell blank as she tried to assimilate this information. "So…so, there's no man involved? No father?"

She fell into the chair next to Lily, amazement marking her features.

"No, no father. And Flynn's not really a man—or a woman—just energy."

"Will wonders never cease," Hunter muttered, scrubbing one palm across her face and the back of her neck. "I was terrified all this time of actually telling you how I felt, not absolutely sure of your…persuasion." She laughed a short, barking laugh. "Well, I'll be damned."

She looked at Lily's abdomen. "Energy baby. I'll be damned," she repeated, her voice awestricken.

Lily frowned and held her abdomen protectively. "Yes, yes, she is."

Hunter awoke to Lily's possible hurt and indignation. "Oh, sweetheart! I didn't mean anything by that. I'm just amazed is all. She's going to be wonderful, perfect. Our little girl."

She took Lily's hand and kissed it just as Sage entered through the back door. Sage's keen eyes missed nothing, but she spoke as though nothing had changed. "You two need to clear on out so I can get the bread started for dinner. Get on with you." She lifted a dishtowel and made shooing motions at them.

Lily and Hunter rose and spoke in unison. "Yes, Saysay."

They laughed at one another as they left the kitchen together.

EVENT HORIZON

"It's odd to realize, isn't it?" Hunter mused quietly. "I think about it when I'm driving to work sometimes."

She was in the chair next to their bed in the master bedroom. One warm palm rested on Lily's forearm, the other on Lily's cramping abdominal muscles. "You know, that they do exist. Like there's this whole hidden world that we knew nothing about, aliens and interdimensional energy beings. That no one else knows about. It just boggles my mind."

Lily nodded and moaned again as her body tried to bring Aili out into the world. She was five hours into labor and the contractions of her uterus were causing the pain from her wounded legs to flare up.

"I try not to think about it. Makes me wonder what else is out there that we don't know anything about," she said and then gasped in pain, both hands on her belly.

"Are you really, really sure you want to have the baby here? The hospital is a much better place for this," Hunter asked once more in an urgent whisper, her brow furrowed with worry. "Especially with first babies. And after what you've been through…"

Lily cried out helplessly as Sage entered the room with a cup of ice chips. Sage set it aside and took Lily's hand in her good one. "This too shall pass, Little Lil. Your body is still strong. Let the body work."

"I've had enough of hospitals," Lily muttered, eyes fixed on Hunter.

She gasped as a strong buzzing hum rattled through her. It sounded and felt like a swarm of bees inside her.

Hunter and Sage both felt it and looked pointedly at Lily's abdomen. Hunter sighed and rolled her eyes before placing both palms on that abdomen to gauge the baby's location. "She is moving down nicely with each contraction. Keep it up, Lil."

Lily smiled apologetically to Sage, then devoted every bit of strength and energy she could muster toward bringing her daughter into the light of day. She had been and was seriously still worried about the appearance of the baby, but there was no turning back now. At least Sage and Hunter, who both loved her, might accept it if her baby had bright silver eyes and white hair.

Two hours later, she berated herself for her fears. A beautiful human infant rested in her arms, looking up at her with crystal blue eyes. Wise eyes, but human.

"Hello, Aili," she said, once she'd caught her breath. "Welcome to New Mexico."

Aili smiled and wriggled in her mother's arms.

Bella Books, Inc.

Women. Books. Even Better Together.

P.O. Box 10543
Tallahassee, FL 32302

Phone: 800-729-4992
www.bellabooks.com